I DIDN'T MEAN TO BE KEVIN

CALEB J. ROSS

Viscera

Irrational

Also by Caleb J. Ross

Stranger Will: a novel
Charactered Pieces: stories
Murmurs: Gathered Stories Vol. One
As a Machine and Parts: a novella

Originally published by Black Coffee Press, 2012, 2nd edition, 2013
Viscera Irrational

Cover design and internal layout, Caleb J. Ross
Cover image spxChrome via iStockPhoto.com

ISBN-13: 978-0615954097

Produced in the United States of America

To all the lost children out there...

ONE

I Know Marion Garza

*T*his guy, Marion Garza, torched blood at the BWP plant anytime the incinerator broke down, but he never complained; it wasn't as intensive as his normal gig: slicing necks above the floor drain, a thatched metal grill referred to around the meat plant as "the gateway". What happens is, after a herd moves up the ramp through the giant yellow door, each cow is strapped into a harness and ushered over a retractable floor. When the floor falls away the cow is left hovering. This lessens its struggle and allows the stunner to get close enough to knock the bitch through the skull. BLAM! Think of a pneumatic power nailing gun, only the size of a small cannon. Right between the eyes. Fourteen hours a day. To maintain mental stability a stunner works in six-week rotating shifts with enough time off between to fill his head with something other than the haunting visual of a last spray from the dying facial artery pulse.

Sometimes the product doesn't die immediately.

"Nervous twitching," the PR people tell local newspapers to curb the aftershock of a disgruntled worker venting to the wrong person at the wrong bar after ending an especially brutal shift. "Just nerves still pulsing through the brain. They can't feel anything." To the PR group, to the public, words calm. To Marion Garza the "nervous twitching" has resulted in a broken maxilla, thirteen stitches along his right bicep, bruised ribs, and a cracked bicuspid. The cauliflower ear, however, he claims is a badge from his years as a semi-pro boxer in Chihuahua. You'd believe him with arms like his.

To stabilize a panicked animal Marion Garza has a single option: fight. To keep production high, the belts moving, he isn't allowed to call the stunner over for a second shot. His only option is to control the inverted animal—it swinging by cracking legs on a hook riding an overhead trolley—until he can hold the head still enough for a good slice through the aorta. His station really is the last resort. After necking, the animal rolls onto a belt manned on each side by workers; eight arms at once separate the cow. Injuries here could dent human capital enough for prices to shift at supermarkets.

No more nervous twitching after Marion Garza. Fourteen hours a day he does this getting home just in time to microwave a Pop-Tart and fall to the couch. He showers occasionally.

But when the incinerator breaks the plant pulls

Marion Garza to the collecting pool at the end of the gateway's route. Here, he perfumes the air of the city with burning blood. He stands knee-deep, sweeping its surface with a reconditioned World War II man-portable M2A1-7 flame thrower modified with duel static tanks while fans behind him blow the spent air out into the world. Don't think pollution. Think community.

Marion Garza is a quiet man and despite the roaring machines and constant hum of rotary saws through bone, the solitude suits him. Silence, even relative silence, is a luxury. Flaming the blood pool, he gets silence more than any other worker.

Most plants truck in cattle, right up to the ramps, from feedlots and backgrounding pens states away. BWP prides itself in being one of the only packing plants in the entire country to have both lots onsite. In backgrounding pens the cattle are taught to eat corn, problematic in many ways—the toxicity of the Rumensin injections given to ward off infections during grain introduction weakens their stomachs; or their liver is shot within months; or they develop acidosis; or when the Rumensin fails the cattle bloats which essentially suffocates them from the inside by expanding the stomach against the lungs—but corn is economical. In the feed lots they eat for mass gain. All corn. Only the lead cow, El Niño, gets grass.

For a while BWP employed, a prodder instead of a lead steer, a man who spent his days at the feedlot zapping the animals into an organized and obedient line, managing the herds up the ramp, through the giant yellow door opening to the kill shed. Realizing this may be a waste of money, the powers decided to train a single cow that could not only lead the rest up the ramp peacefully, but could calm the animals pre-killing-shed by setting an example, becoming a leader for the pack in a "look at my healthy coat and composed demeanor—don't worry—they're alright people" kind of way. This is El Niño. They call her a Judas Cow. She eats grass and sleeps between shows.

After fourteen hours a man without a name steps in to take over the torch. Marion Garza times his exit, punching the clock, removing overcoats, changing boots, and on to his late model Ford Festiva before the sun has a chance to reveal the proof of a new day. A hang-up anywhere means acknowledging for a brief instant the reality of the backgrounding pen and the feedlot and of El Niño, ignorant at the center of everything.

Outside, the stiff morning breeze brings with it the strong smell of oil and stressed brakes.

At home Marion Garza microwaves a hamburger. He watches Telemundo, a channel he hates, and falls asleep in his chair, the empty plate resting on his stomach.

When he wakes, the setting sun peeks through a hole in the aluminum foil taped to his west window. Unable to find more foil he patches the opening with a silver gum wrapper, using the gum as an adhesive. He eats a bowl of cereal, drinks a microwaved cup of coffee left over from the evening before. During the drive he wonders how the foil might have torn away, why his home seems to be breaking during the night.

The next shift, with the incinerator still broken Marion Garza takes the torch from the man without a name and nods as he turns away. Sweat drips from underneath the white hardhat, it feels like dripping plastic, like slow petrifaction from the head down.

For lunch Marion Garza escapes to the roof with a cigarette and the subtle beginnings of a smile eager to justify his happiness with the cool breezes above.

The sun digs underneath him. For miles this small city is a grid of sporadic street lights celebrating the absent sun. Marion Garza inhales deep, taking in smoke and the stink of manure that fills the north pens. It will be cleaned in another three months, between backgrounding classes, but for now it floats ripe, almost visible in the air. Through his tight wool hat he can hear the erratic mooing climbing up from the pens below. But he doesn't look. He just pretends the wails are a song of the hills, the sounds of a view he pretends to have chosen.

When Marion Garza was born his mother loved him enough to hide him in a garbage bag. She kissed him through the black plastic, unsure if she connected with a cheek, a head, an arm, or a shoe, then nestled him into her brother's trunk before the man made his annual tour of the southwest selling used clothing at gas stations. Marion Garza's mother died two months later from mastitis in her left breast.

Standing at the top of a beef packing plant he can see far enough into the horizon to know the curvature of the earth, far enough to acknowledge his own back as the land comes around behind him, but not far enough to look beyond the possibility that his mother may have made the wrong choice. The land stretches only so far.

Creeping down the scaffolding Marion Garza keeps his eyes narrow, blurring the world. He feels his way along the wall, steps high over possible stones or ill-placed tools. But despite these devices he can still hear El Niño quietly shifting cud. Even above the approaching trucks El Niño grunts contention. She is a bright white blur no matter how much Marion Garza wants her dim.

When Marion Garza trips over hidden train tracks, and falls to the ground, the animal turns away and lumbers to the furthest corner of her private pen. From there she drops to the grass and stares. Night and dawn Marion Garza must endure this ignorant beast for the few moments he has between his car and the necking pit. She is bright with healthy blood, free from the manure the other animals wear as coats. A true lifer.

He drives a screwdriver through El Niño's left eye. A man near the ramp witnesses the act, yells, but

Marion doesn't stop.

The stabbing wasn't pity. Don't think pity. Marion isn't one to feel sorry for anybody for any reason. It wasn't about cruelty or liberation or food. It wasn't a rule he finally brought to practicality or a lesson he had been taught and only then understood. It wasn't about punishment either. He never believed in punishment—a false concept that breeds fear where paths fork. Make a decision and worship it. Let the congregation deal with the consequences. No. Maiming El Niño was probably more of a control thing. Or a revelation. Whatever it was, it was entirely personal. Nobody but that man saw Marion Garza attack El Niño. And if connections can be made, the man found dead in the back of a locked semi-trailer last spring, starved to bones with a screwdriver through his temple, could very well be that man.

I know Marion Garza.

TWO

Creg Deja's Ugly Mother

"**B**ullshit."

"Bullshit?"

"Bullshit."

So, he didn't believe me. I play appalled, but I'm not. What really is the point of repeating a believable story? And although I accept his denial I still wish he would take the story of Marion Garza as the warning it is meant to be. "Really, I know him."

Creg lays down his pen. "No. The rest of it. None of that shit happened."

Creg Deja has a tough time trusting anyone. I don't blame him. Like me, he was abandoned at an early age by unsuitable parents. He spends his days searching for his mother, his nights destroying laundromats. Whatever takes the edge off, I suppose.

"It happened, man," I say stuffing away selection F2, Snyder's Hotdog flavored potato chips, into the vending machine, without regard for expiration dates. Creg shakes his head and yawns, looking back to the TV set bolted above us. The stretch of his neck and point of his chin imply prayer. I repeat the climax spacing the words by seconds: "He—stabbed—the—bitch."

Closing his notebook—a rare gesture—Creg stands, reaches above me, and increases the TV volume so loud the cracked speaker vibrates the entire vending machine top row of Nut Roll bars. Luisa, the owner of this aptly named Luisa's Laundry, flashes a quick frown my way. She begins to speak, but instead exits into the back. Creg reopens his notebook, a marbled black and white composition pad, worn to fibers after these long weeks of use.

"I'm telling you. If you find your mom you don't want her working there. It fucks with people. They had Marion on six week rotations because of how it affects the head." Creg pulls his eyes from the screen for a quick second, drops them dismissively on me.

"*When* I find her." he says.

"I know," I say. "I know. Should have been four weeks."

Spitting shards of a comped beef jerky stick all over his notebook, he says, "That's just a last resort thing, anyway. She could probably get some acting stuff up here. Latinas are trendy, you know."

By *here* he means the U.S., not this particular barrio. Veranda is like a trap people know exists, but still venture into anyway. Flashing lights, bilingual signs, warning pamphlets mailed to every address from here to Sedna, twice—it wouldn't matter what precautions slaves like me might take to keep people out, they'll flock one day, like cattle. And by *acting* I assume he means porn. Although, I hope not. And judging by the looks of the headshot he keeps folded in his wallet, I'm not sure even three degrees of separation—a director, a camera, a poor TV set—is enough distance to keep human eyes from what might lie below. And besides being ugly, she was a bitch, too.

"Fuck," he yells, as an incoming customer pushes through the door. "I just missed every single fucking name."

He's referring to the end credits of *Bienvendidos a la Mañana*.

For a while I did more with my life than fill vending machines. I used to moonlight for the Missing Children's Network pasting grainy-faced mosaic posters and flyers around town. It was an honorable enough job until an unfortunate incident involving my removal of random photos, a felled tree branch, and parent with a stronger swing than her appearance would imply forced my resignation. I won't admit guilt, but I will stand in defense of the real culprit—none of those kids were coming back alive anyway. And via this pessimism I met Creg.

I remember the first conversation with Creg, not long after the branch to my head. "You think they find any of them?"

I remember my reply clearly: "Nope."

For a few weeks my visits to Luisa's Laundry fell into a stalemate, those first words being the only ones we shared. I'd top out a row of Butterfingers while enduring a laugh track. I'd clean the front glass and hear Creg mumble about facial features and hair color. But one afternoon, over a shared cigarette, I asked him about the notebook.

"That for school or something?"

"No."

"Writing a book?"

"No."

"Making a hit-list?"

A longer pause, then a long sigh. "No."

I sat for a moment peeking at an open page. Though, it was illegible, with quick scratches and tight scribbles, I could barely make out a catalog of physical attributes. Eye color, shape, skin color, hair style, and crude sketches for pages and pages. I had to ask again. "Making a hit-list?"

He pulled out that folded headshot and said, "It's my mom."

It was old, faded, deteriorated at the edges and stained all the colors of dirt and sweat. But the paper's condition paled in contrast for the portrait itself. Like I said, Creg's mother was ugly.

"Nice," I said, trying to sound sincere.

He pointed to her signature in the lower corner of the headshot. "She kissed that spot before signing it," he says. "Last thing she said to me was to keep the picture safe. 'This autograph will put you through college one day she said."

Creg's mother left him. One day she grabbed her cigarettes and announced her plans to be a telenovela Soap star in Mexico. She didn't even know Spanish. Her boyfriend knew a little. This fact does not deter Creg from false hope, but rather, he holds a faith stronger than logic. What about the father? Died when Creg was young. A taboo subject all together. He doesn't talk about his death because as he puts it, "I don't know his death."

In many ways I feel sorry for Creg. I pity Creg for his delusions; but I admire his dedication. He's been here every afternoon I have, filling reams of paper with detail upon detail. Somewhere behind all the flash, behind the laugh tracks and the gratuitous dancing and all those Telemundo close-ups lives Creg's mother. In each storyline and performance, in each plot development and twist that to other viewers might pull attention away from a mole or a crooked smile, Creg found hope in exactly those unique flaws.

"It's like the role of the makeup artist is to keep families apart," he said.

"Maybe I could help," I suggested. "I'm Mexican."

He turned from the screen and inspected my face with a sharp stare. "You're not Mexican. You don't know Spanish."

"Sure I am. It's in my blood."

And with that he broke a smile. Not my intention, but it was worth it. To fool a person out of. spite is to fool yourself. To fool a person out of pleasure is—I don't remember how it goes.

The sun is harsh today, moving chocolate like loose mud inside candy bar wrappers. For almost a year now, I've known Creg and not even heat like this fails to keep him away from this TV, this laundromat.

Killing the empty jerky wrapper in a white-knuckled fist, Creg inhales twice, deep, and tries to shake the feeling back into his hand, preparing for a *Sábado Gigante* rerun.

Luisa and Creg have an agreement. He can watch all the Spanish TV he wants. He can control the channel, the volume, and after thirteen notebooks he's just sort of fallen into the privilege of doing anything he wants, really.

And in return all Creg has to do is help Luisa advertise her laundromat. Un-advertise might be a better description. Under mild criticism he would be called a petty vandal. Some might blame him for job loss, bankruptcy, increased insurance premiums, perpetuating gang violence. This last accusation stemming from his most creative endeavor—my idea by the way—faking gang graffiti, hence property destroyed, real estate value dropped, and blame displaced.

All of it is just subversive attempts to bring Luisa ever closer to citywide laundering dominance. He cuts listings for other cleaners from telephone books, from every newspaper in a five block radius of Luisa's Laundry. *Product displacement*, he calls it.

During commercials he alternates between cutting full color ads from free local shopper papers with quickly scribbled descriptions of onscreen action. He searches the credits for a new name his mother may have adopted. Then he'll work on a draft for a letter to the editor of *The Veranda View* regarding the Chinese laundry in uptown, warning potential customers of *depraved conditions and poor quality* in hopes of disabling the competition. He ends that letter with *they're not even Chinese, they're Korean*, unsure if the owners really are. Accuracy doesn't matter; his perpetuated hope for finding his mother blinds him from all else. He could probably find easier ways of getting Spanish TV but honestly, I think he stays for Luisa. They share moments. I've noticed even if they haven't. When he senses progress, she works harder. When he gets discouraged, she slows her pace to give the moment entirely to him. She cares, I think because she understands no one else does. She has children of her own, yes, obligations outside the laundry, but a mother preys on unconditional need. I've learned to fill the machine on Tuesdays and Fridays between twelve-fifteen and twelve-thirty because she brings sandwiches. One for Creg out of sympathy. One for me out of pity. I'm fine with it. I'll eat pity. She's a little late for a Tuesday, but Creg doesn't know this. She hands Creg a brown sack, offering a compassionate smile with it, and to me she tosses a bag and rolls her eyes. "Thanks," I say. Creg eats, his eyes still searching the screen.

"You can try to keep her away from BWP," ham paste falls from my mouth, "but it won't work."

"She's not like your mother. She has drive."

I pause. "You've never even met my mother."

"I didn't mean it that way."

"She has drive," I repeat, taking a bite of the sandwich. Onions on an Asiago bun— gross—I turn to Lisa. "Why do you like Creg more than me?"

"He's got drive."

My smile fades.

Creg drifts back to the TV. A family of four scatters into the laundry, each member straining under the weight of a designated shoulder-slung bag. The parents secure a small fleet of washers along the north wall while the children immediately attack a *Snow Brothers* video game in the corner. They fight over first player.

"All I'm saying is that if you do find her and she does come back, she'll be pulled into working at BWP. They all do." The arcade machine suddenly illuminates. A theme song sounds, further enticing the children.

"*I* don't work there," he says. He eyes me like he's discovered something. "A job is a job. You hate yours."

"No," I say without even thinking of other possible responses. "It's cool. Pretty much."

Creg shakes his head. Even Luisa contributes another eye roll.

"No, really," I say to both of them, even to the observing family I feel I need to impress. "The trick is to remind yourself that you are helping people to push on a little longer. A snack here, a snack there. Sometimes a triple fudge brownie roll is all someone needs."

"Why does there have to be a trick, Jackson?"

And with that he shuts me up. I won't and never will claim to love my job. I've never, however, claimed to hate it. But I see Creg's point. Dream jobs are just that—dreams—and I would offer this clever witticism if it weren't for validating Creg's argument. So what if he finds his mother? So what if she agrees to move back to America? So what if she is forced to cut necks at BWP? A job is a job and judging by the lack of success Creg is having with finding his mother I'd say she hasn't realized her dream either. But vending isn't so bad, really. I get to talk to interesting people, I'm not imprisoned within a cubicle, and I get all the chocolate Moon Pies I want.

Creg sketches a woman's face; he circles the full cheeks and makes arrows to highlight her gapped teeth, just like the gap-toothed smile of his mother. "Should you really have to rely on a *trick* to be happy?"

Yes, I want to say. I want to point out his attempts, his coming here every day to stalk this fading idea of happiness. And fade it will until it vanishes. I worry what Creg will become once he acknowledges this inevitability. I can guess. But instead I ask, "What does happiness have to do with a job?" A child walks up with change a nickel short of the Gobstoppers he reaches for. I tell him to look behind the toilet for more money, but as the kid turns Creg pulls out a nickel. The child buys his candy but still moves to the bathroom on his hands and knees.

Ignoring my original question I ask another, feigning a passing thought: "Why do you want to find her anyway?"

"Next week she will have been gone for...," he says.

"Mine's been gone longer," I say.

"It's not a competition."

"It should be," I say. "I'd be a pro. Endorsements and everything. Sponsors would pay me to product-place during couch sessions with a camera-friendly therapist."

Luisa leaves the front counter for the back room. I close and lock the vending machine.

"All these years without a phone call," I say. "Why not even a single phone call?"

Behind our silence driers hum, children laugh,

and the two parents read separate magazines, alternating twisted glances to the TV.

"She'll call," he says.

"Right," is all I can say. I pack the remaining snacks tight, wrap what's left of my sandwich into a small bundle, and ask Creg if he needs a ride home.

"I rode my bike."

I shout my goodbyes and thanks back to Luisa. She doesn't respond.

With one hand at the door Creg calls my name. "Honestly, you never think about yours."

"Sure," I say. I think about my mother making dinner. I think about my mother prepping for a Friday night out, celebrating some anniversary—a marriage, an election to city council, my departure. I think of her tending the home, organizing Mary Kay parties, planning Don Ho and Dean Martin playlists for neighborhood housewives. I wonder if this is really what a mother does, or have I been warped by TV and residual interactions here at Luisa's. I wonder how it would feel to not wonder anymore, but instead I say only, "Sure, sometimes," like I haven't spent so many hours of my life exploring this very question.

"I wish you understood," he says. "I wish you didn't piss away at life, living like the past didn't exist. I came from somewhere, Jackson. I came from someone and until I find her again I can't pretend that a night without a phone call means I was never born."

Two hands to the door: "Yeah you can." And the bell rings loud above my head. Instead of covering my ear I grab a newspaper from the rack at my side and wonder who might have been fired since scanning the want-ads yesterday morning.

THREE

I Know Kevin Masons

Bold. Important. Screaming to be noticed. DRIVERS the heading announces followed by columns filled with tight black text. Cross country freight, lumber transportation, owner operators preferred, round-trip dedicated runs, local routes, and even an ad for a four week CDL training program for those like me from a few years ago. I fell into the promise of good money— "Team oriented" it required and who is more team oriented than me? I could rally no matter the cause. The want-ads go on, but a hole, one of Creg's laundry ad removals, taken from the center of the page, prevents me from reading on. The missing space cuts into the DRIVERS heading starting from the ELECTRICIAN heading at the right. Creg told me that Sparkle Clean, a new competing laundry in South Town, had been advertising for a part-time handyman in the ELECTRICIAN heading for the last three weeks to take care of malfunctioning washers. Creg showed me these missing ads. "No electrician, no handyman ever could clean out all the sand I dumped in there," he told me, tossing the ads into an overflowing trashcan. When he told Luisa not to worry about Sparkle Clean anymore she smiled all pride. I wish I could say the sand was my idea, but Creg has become his own genius over the months. I envy his direction. His drive.

Transportation companies promote life on the open road. I never believed I was the right person, but even fuckups have to pay bills. I took the class, passed barely, and was on the road the following day learning a route I couldn't forget now no matter how many others I've traveled. And here's a full page more. GreenAmerica has a new listing today for a loader down at distribution. Looks like they finally caught Tim masturbating into glue bottles. Tim needed to move on anyway.

I could get a new job, learn new scenery, but what really would change? *There is nothing new under the sun*, I read somewhere, and the more I think about it the more I agree. Everything has been here since the beginning. We've just found more creative methods of exploitation.

Take for instance this florist ad:

Floral Designer
Full time or part time.
Experience necessary.
Must have portfolio

*including photographs.
Inquire with resume
and portfolio at the
Shadeville office.*

Ignoring for a moment the pompous use of "Floral Designer" in place of the more traditional "Florist," let's examine the shallow pool of possible candidates: Old women, gay men. I'm neither. You've got to know the lingo, and no way will they train you. Old women spend years watching gardening shows, and years more cultivating dirt, like they're prepping for their own eternal stay, and I'm asked to be on par with that? And gay men love controlling nature. It's sort of a spit in the face of heterosexuality and our life-creating ways. Which returns to my original argument: Just let the flowers grow. No need to bastardize nature with a human-centric egotism. It's not often that nature harms independently of human interference. Animals, weather, and earthquakes. Other than that, Mother Nature pays about as much attention as Mother Jacoby.

But don't dub me a tree-hugger yet. I drove Maple Creek log shipments for a few weeks before sliding over to GreenAmerica. I was drawn to the benefits mostly and figured I could improvise the "courteous and qualified" part. Turns out I couldn't. The dispatcher, an overweight bear named Roe hated me from the start. Five weeks in and I exploded, sending Roe to the hospital with a mild concussion and barely enough motor skill left to sign my pink slip. Courteous is relative, anyway.

On down the line a manly sounding job jumps out at me:

MACHINIST
Exp operating Punch Press and Forklift.
All Shifts
Must lift 50lbs.
Temp-hire
Phone number below. Ask for Bill.

Fifty pounds—sure. Temp-position—sure. Punch Press—how hard can it be? I give Bill a call and tell him the ad caught my attention. Not because of my qualifications but because of the center justification. "Most of the other ads are right-justified." He dodges a response by reciting the ad almost verbatim: "You have experience operating a Punch Press and forklift...you can work any shift...you can lift"... and so on. I say "yeah" to everything until he offers an interview for tomorrow at eleven thirty. "I can't," I say. "I have a funeral," and I hang up. He was too trusting.

A telephone relationship isn't like any other relationship; all you have is voice. And not even pure voice, but a representation of sorts filtered through wires and cables and plastic. I did some telemarketing work my last year of high school. The softest, most pleasant "hello" often ended in threats because of trust. I'd get too close. That's what the managers told me. I'd graduate from using last names to using firsts to exploring hobbies to talk of weekend activities. Before I knew it the supervisors would cut the line and call me back into the office. They kept me on longer than they should have, for a few more calls ending in only a few different ways. I thought I knew voice until that job. Now I know that voice can be just another desperate criminal.

I've been working my whole life. As a child, before my father died, I helped him build houses. I'd pick up nails from the grass and clean tools mostly, but with my tiny brain I truly believed that together we were creating something important. After he died my mother sold the contracting business to a couple from somewhere out east. Iowa, or something. All of these associations with my father's business return hard as I scan the ads further down the page.

An ad for a Welder Helper under LABOR brings it all back—perform a combination of duties to assist workers, familiar with brazing, experienced arc cutting, can lift heavy weight repeatedly, and on down the list in a column duel-justified, text-wrapped, and packed so tight with words the ad looks like a solid brick of steel bracing the paper. *Applications must have proof of legal authority to work in the United States.* This last bit is something my father neglected once in favor of compassion.

When I was young, during a residential build miles outside a town even maps ignore, my father brought an outside welder on-site to fine tune some erroneously cut supports for a basement ceiling. Bringing a welder on-site wasn't a common practice for many reasons, but from what I remember my father was never one to obey rules. During the cut, sparks flying and the entire crew entranced, I wandered close to the heat. I remember how amazing it looked, so much fire so far from the Fourth of July. I made my way closer, closer, sliding up behind the man with mask. He swung back, "scared," he said later, and down I went suffering not only a nail through the back of the head but a deep burn from the welder's dropped torch. My left ear, gone, has been replaced by a smooth graft of skin, but I'm still deaf to the world on that side of my head.

Anything I remember from that stretch of time is warped by an idyllic mental state which now, needing such an edge softener, I absolutely cannot regain. I'd let that day happen in my head over and over, I float through each moment. I have troubles to this day. I get headaches when I get nervous and my vision gives when the temperature rises.

And I would wander a lot, my absences growing by hours, sometimes days. A quick trip to the corner gas station would end in my return three days later with a soda and an unopened beef stick. My mother called the police the first time it happened. By the fifth time, the routine of my disappearances made ignoring my absence easy; I was on my own even then.

Streetlights shine down through my bedroom window, cutting the felled evening like a dull butter knife. Pulling the paper close in the dim light I filter through so many want ads.

Every evening I look through these ads and think, "I have the drive. I have the desire. I can sell doughnuts or vacuum cleaners or whatever else they want me to peddle," knowing that in reality all three claims are false. But I keep looking.

It's been my experience that if a job title is created by adding -*er* to the duty it's a tough job to admit having—pastry stuffer, housekeeper, necker, vending machine filler, truck driver.

I circle an ad for a soccer instructor under RECREATION but kill the thing with heavy ink when I read "min rqmt: Ass deg." Then on to: **Fire Safety Dealer Rep**: Ambitious leader needed to secure brand in new market. New patented product line. Full training. Two seminars per month. *Who wouldn't want to invest in fire safety*, I ask. *Me*, I answer. **Dental Assistant and Front Desk Receptionist wanted at Condel Dentistry**: Exp. FT/PT. Great Benefits. Friendly staff. I begin a tight neon-pink highlight through this one but pull away when I reread "Friendly staff." Boasting like this means a hidden lie. And what would they think of me? Would they accept me? Would they invite me to happy-hour? Or would they take one look at my scarred ear and say "no, we're just going home tonight." Or would they be compassionate and I only twist the words into disinterest because nothing gets through my broken ear.

Page after page of desperate employers reach out, make promises, entice, and day after day new crops find new eyes and new lives embrace new concerns, new doubts, new ways to hate themselves. This barber I once knew, Ferguson or something, said that a job is what people get when they stop loving themselves. I tipped him five dollars for that line, sacrificing coffee money for the following week.

So Creg might be right. Maybe I do hate my job.

The evening has devolved into night. With my uniform still sweating to my thighs and chest I drop the newspaper and retire to the bathroom for a quick jerk and long shower. The mirror steams and I leave it that way, uncaring as to how my hair has decided to fall. Then back to the newspaper.

A want-ad, two columns wide catches my eye—an unusual size, atypical placement, and all-around unfamiliar.

Help Wanted
SKILLED LABOR
Kevin Masons

All my fault. I cnt begin to expr. how sry I am for all. Pls come home. U R all I want. Father is sry, too. If U wld just call we cld talk about evrythng. We've ben lonely w/o U. 6 yrs is a long tme 2 B gone. We jst want to know U R ok. Pls call and let us hav 1 night of sound sleep. You bles our dreams. Waking trs us aprt. We still live at home and wll keep a lite on 4 U. ALSO, skilled laborer wanted. Pls call home, Kevin...

I read it twice. It's an ad I've never seen. I tear out the ad out and tuck away the folded plea. Creg will shit when he reads this.

I look down to the resulting hole in the center once occupied by the ad, all else moving toward it like some tiny black hole right there on my living room floor. The empty space reveals ads for security jobs, for railroad grinders, hospice workers, fast food, and more sales positions, characters tight like a single block of black paint. Kevin Masons—a boy whose search starts at this center of everything, a desperate black hole born of a desperate mother.

Kevin Masons. A nomad probably, though I'd guess educated. Educated enough to read. Maybe cheap, too, if frugality is genetic. Papers charge by the letter, after all.

I could envy this boy for what he might never know, could wish I might one day open a newspaper to "Jackson Jacoby" in bold serif, but I won't. I don't believe my mother regrets our situation enough spend that kind of cash.

Knowing enough about the familial disputes I can't help but side with Kevin, disregarding the fact that I shouldn't care enough to side at all. But I've been there. I've endured what three school counselors termed *out of my league*, and suffered for each visit bruises, drugged sleep, and *something worth crying about*. Kevin Mason is solitary now, and should we ever walk the same street I'd pass by, offering only a wink. Motherless guys like us, we are our own mothers.

The night is guided by streetlights and rare headlights but it's a young Wednesday night, and I need something to abort this festering idea of Kevin Masons. I leave for the bar, tying my shoes as I hop to the GreenAmerica truck.

FOUR

The Ear I Stole

*T*his guy I know, Marion Garza, had no
family so when he stopped cutting necks
and started driving trucks he had nobody
to fill his thoughts, nothing to look forward to but the
perpetual horizon ahead.

He rode the hum of tires tearing from dark asphalt
with all the somber optimism of a life built to reach
this very moment. When children pumped their arms,
tugging on imaginary air horns from backseats of
passing Volvos he'd sound his horn and enjoy their
faces. His smile frightened children, so he stopped. He
just let the children slide down their seats and fall
back into their beautiful lives.

He'd always been a self-contained man, finding
happiness where it found him—in the open doorways
of strangers. He'd smile only when the world around
him allowed the display, when a woman thanked him
for a propped door, when another driver offered the
salt from his table. And on the rare occasion that a lot
lizard approached his truck to trade companionship

for a small amount of money.

This one's name was Dynasty, born Gina as Marion Garza would learn later over hot chocolate and a slice of lemon meringue pie. She didn't demand the courtship, but he offered knowing the guilt he'd wake to the following morning should he not spend those few extra moments pretending they didn't understand each other's motives, like they were two real people doing real people things. He learned somewhere to be gentle with a woman, even one with thigh-high boots armed with heels that, if driven by enough anger, could aerate a stomach.

I stop and take a long look around this basement bar, ending on Tracey's boots, nodding, saying "like those," and finish with a wink. I swing back into the story:

With one bite left of the lemon meringue the lizard sets her fork on the table and tells Marion Garza that she'd prefer the dome light off. "It's not the ear," she says, unprovoked, though her gaze remains fixed.

He smiles and fills his mouth with her last bit of pie, then throws a few bills on the table and escorts the woman out the truck stop door.

On the way to his truck, his teeth clicking in the cold, the lizard grabs him by the crotch and says, "I'll warm you," but releases when she trips. She blames a rock. Marion Garza helps her to her feet, and offers all sympathy, though he looks back to see no such offending rock. The asphalt exists, in fact, as one of the only reliably supportive structures for miles.

In the cab she takes a quick look to the dashboard clock. Marion Garza says, "It's cold," and unzips his pants only enough to pull himself out. He hides his cock with the tail of his shirt. He reaches up to the dome light, but the lizard stops him, says "wait," and grabs at his cauliflower ear. She asks its history, genuinely interested even as she pulls up her skirt, shifting it like skin from her legs. Her boots she keeps fastened.

"I was a fighter," he lies and stares beyond her eager eyes, searching for a memory. In Chihuahua, he claims, he was a pit boxer for a number of years earning what he could to repay debts incurred throughout a life land-marked by bad decisions. He'd borrow money from distant relatives, shady friends, and acquaintances who knew enough to lend only what they themselves had stolen. Most of the people he fought to repay were contacts severed years ago, but for personal reasons, he claims, he worked to pay off debts even if the money went straight back into a shot-glass. And he was good; a good fighter, and a damn good liar.

"Like Johnny Truant."

"Who?" Tracey asks.

"Forget it," I say and continue with the story:

Marion Garza reaches again for the dome light. Again, the lizard stops him, this time caressing the mangled ear. She traces its trenches and mountains, its billows like clouds, with a soft touch and a contorted face. "Fighting, huh?" Her finger leaves a wake of goose-bumps and nervous sweat.

Marion Garza yawns, embarrassed by his growing erection, unable to stop it like he is unable to stop the girl from warming his face. "Grappling, mostly," he says slowly filling with pride. Few people he'd let touch his ear: a doctor, once, an old girlfriend, supervised children, and a woman he thought might lend him a few bucks for the privilege. Gina, the newest of the privileged, he allows for two reasons: one, she does it so well, and two the cab doors are locked.

"I've got to tell you, Mari," she says, "I'm a little bit jealous," and with that he smiles enough to forget his embarrassment.

The lizard clicks off the dome light, despite stubborn light from a nearby streetlight. She lays back, looks again to the dashboard clock, and spreads herself open while chewing at her red bottom lip.

When Marion Garza shifts to remove her boots she kicks him away. "Leave them on. You'll like it better," she says.

Within minutes the two are drinking from a three dollar bottle of wine and smoking laced grass from Gina's purse with a roach clip fashioned from one of her barrettes, leaving her hair as lopsided as her walk. The last thing Marion Garza feels is the lizard's smooth hand over his ear and his own smile stretched beyond the limits of recent memory.

He wakes hours later, the passenger window broken; his eyes burn beneath a shallow pool of blood. His own blood, Gina's blood, swimming together and spilling down his cheek as Gina shakes him, screaming, yelling about a man with a knife. "He ran that way," she yells and points out into the still-black night surrounding them.

Marion Garza, even drunk and high, knows the taste of his own blood and fears what he might find should he investigate its source. Gina is still shaking him by the collar and swings her legs around to reveal a nub dripping with deep red.

"My foot!" she yells through mascara tears.

"Christ," Marion yells and can feel the pain in his head before the word ends. He leans up to the rearview mirror finding his head red where his cauliflower ear once existed. "My ear," he says sweeping the rest of his body for more.

"You've got to go after him," Gina yells, digging through the peeled layers of discarded pants and shirts until she finds something to wrap her wound with. Finding nothing, she forces her boots over the wound and throws a shirt at Marion telling him to hurry or "you'll never get your ear back."

They panic. The girl screams about her foot. Marion tries to understand his new face by the streetlight light and rearview mirror. He eventually grabs his keys and starts the truck, unsure where he intends to go and what he intends to do once he gets *there. He knows, though, that a parking lot can no longer suffice as a safe home.*

"We'll find him," Gina says spit-shaping her hair in a sun visor mirror.

Marion Garza still dabs his ear, and blood spills from his eye-sill like red tears. Gina pulls out a bottle of Vicodin, throws it to Marion's lap, and tells him that the man shouldn't be too hard to find. He believes her, unsure if finding the man is even the direction he wants to go.

"I got a really good look at him," she says and pulls out an expired lottery ticket and a pen from the floor of the cab, scribbling a stream of words on the ticket's back.

"Brown eyes," I say and open mine wide to Tracey who sits beside me with a fresh bottle of light beer and cigarette pumping smoke between us.

"Brown hair." I point to the top of my head. "Long fingers." I wiggle mine and wink.

She stares at me.

"Maybe a bit of a drinker." I rattle the ice in my empty glass. The bartender heeds the call and arrives with a fresh Coke and Jäger, setting a small bottle of Grenadine beside the glass. "Sharp cheeks." I lean in close to the woman and display my features. I take a quick sip of my drink. *"And a huge cock,"* I say smiling.

Tracey ashes her cigarette over the bar and pulls a drag ten seconds long before driving the ash into a silver tray. "Is all of this supposed to impress me?"

Pretending a touchdown on the TV above the bar angers me I slam my fist down and turn to Tracey. "*Are* you impressed?"

This is Town Royale, a bar that, despite its name, sits in the middle of nowhere under the ruse of a house miles from any neighbors. At one time it was a small farmhouse surrounded by enough cattle to keep the grass black year-round. Now it draws locals and curious travelers by way of its many homemade signs lining the highway: **Two miles to Town. Next Left Town Royale. Cheap Drinks, Cheap Company 'Round back and Downstairs**. The setup is surprisingly professional: three beers on tap, a finished bar, six stools, TVs, music, glowing signs advertising drinks they don't serve, and "usuals" the world pretends to know only because these sad fuckers would never deny a friend. Aside from the washing machine stuffed into the far corner this place could be any bar in any town at any time of day.

"So what? You know this guy who got his ear cut off?"

I down the rest of my drink as the bartender mixes another. "It was *me*," I say. "*I* took his ear."

"*And* the prostitute's foot?"

"This guy was huge," I say stretching my arms wide and raising my shoulders until my neck disappears into the cradle of my chest. "Around him,

37

all you could think about was being small."

She looks at me, eyeing my physique, which I enhance with a sly ab-flex below my loose work shirt. "Bullshit. Your ear is missing so you steal another guy's ear?"

I slam the bar again. "Really, I knew this guy."

"You didn't take his ear," she says then grins a bit. "Then where is it?"

Prepared for this sort of hesitation I throw back a grin of my own and tell her, "Out in my truck. We can go look if you want." This is move one. Move two is getting her off of the bar stool.

"After what you just told me," she says, turning away, shaking an empty bottle I never saw her drink from. I nod to the bartender, point to her empty bottle. "You're crazy."

"I had reasons to take that ear. I don't do it to everyone."

She laughs at her first pull from the new drink, repeats, "You're crazy" and I don't even care that she's ordered an import. Behind me, a guy yells at no one in particular to "turn that fucking shit off."

When I arrived at Town I took one look at this woman sitting alone at the bar and knew she had to have been from Cleaver. And if not from Cleaver then definitely from Grayson. And if not from Grayson then either Goodville, Brackenwood, or Cheston, all of which sat just outside the limits of any mind in Veranda. These towns were foreign to the contentedly ignorant souls imprisoned within this small town, even considering how generally incestuous this entire region is. We're all part of the same gritty soup despite our aversion to co-simmering. The guy, still yelling about the TV, suddenly falls from his stool. The bartender quickly grabs a mop and starts in on the spilled beer.

Despite her origins I knew she had never heard of Veranda. She came from somewhere at the end of our long road, stopping to pee or for directions, staying for a few beers and the chance to feel exotic. And maybe it's the straight black hair, the shirt she wears tucked under her tits, the delicate embrace of a second cigarette dancing among her magic fingers, or her legs, lightly kissing at her thighs that made me forget to ask where she was from. Instead, I buy her beer I can't afford and lie, saying "I don't buy drinks for everyone." She asks my name. I tell her Kevin, the name still fresh on my mind.

"Let's go Kevin," she says without a smile and stands, finishing her drink in a single string of gulps. She grabs my hand and leads me out the door.

The night has cooled enough to keep two people close, but she ignores the pull of the air and walks three steps ahead. I stumble plenty, I'm sure, and maybe even fall a few times, but being so drunk and cold I couldn't feel a bruise or broken bone. One snapshot is me watching the gentle sway of her ass. Another snapshot is me reaching. A third is the woman grabbing me by my elbow and burning me with a cigarette. Intentional or not, I don't care. Her smell carries me past any hostilities.

"You got a key to this thing?" she asks. Maybe we've been standing here for hours.

"I got keys to all kinds of locks," I say and drop the heavy vending ring twice before finally isolating the truck key. The world spins around the two of us, and when I try to hide a soft belch I taste vomit. She doesn't seem to notice the smell.

Once inside the cab I turn the heat high and aim three vents at this beautiful foreigner. Her eyes take everything in: the rubber bands hanging from the rearview mirror vibrating to the angry engine, the thin shifter knob separating the two of us, she spells words in the window fog— "night," "stars," "ear," and opens the glove box before settling into the seat and tuning the radio to a station half-static, half-distant hip-hop. She purses her lips and slouches as though bored. I think mostly of the deep crevasses of her lips, dry and cracked by the heat jets and cold evening. Those lips jut from her face, exploding in red still bright by the dim dashboard lights. What would they feel like? How would they affect my trembling fingers? Then quick like the moment didn't exist I reach over and wipe my hand across those blistering lips.

Before she can qualify that look of hers with words I claim a spider then brush the imaginary escapee from her shoulder. She considers the gesture for a moment then smiles and settles back into the seat.

"So," she says drumming her thighs to the fading song, "this ear of yours."

"Torch accident," I begin a story of faux heroism to justify my missing appendage. I have plans to embrace the chance to tell my tale. But she interrupts: "no. I mean the ear you stole," and it's a good thing because I had nothing beyond, *gee, it's nothing really*.

From underneath the driver's seat I pull out a wooden box, once the package to a cheap watch I remember losing but don't remember ever wearing. Desperate to keep her wide eyes in mine I pretend to fumble with the box. She's dedicated her attention to communion with me. Events like this are seldom, and I want nothing more than to stretch it, to breathe in her perfume, to memorize her presence for any long journeys ahead. I taste the air and take my time. "Sorry," I say, until finally I slide the lid open and pull out the rotting piece. Under the sparse light it resembles a dried fig.

"Don't ask anyone about it though," I say looking over her shoulder, feigning paranoia. "Might as well not say anything at all. Officials deny everything. They don't want copycats."

She accepts the package with a sweaty palm outlined by bright red fingernails.

"The greatest crimes of our time," I say, "few people even know about."

She holds it close to the LED numbers shining from the dashboard.

"To imagine, Charles Manson was a failure in the eyes of the American Government."

She exhales loudly and begins to slip on a jacket I didn't know she had. "This is a wad of gum," she says. "Chewed," and she throws it at me.

"No," I say and turn on the dome light. "It's puffy like that because of a hematoma between the ear cartilage and the skin. So many punches to the head will do that."

She leans back in and grabs for the ear. I refuse to let it go. We share this moment even if only I realize it. "I can see the teeth marks," she says.

"When the clot pushes the skin away from the cartilage it does that. The cartilage doesn't get any nutrients and it dies and shrivels." I'm pointing out this topography, brushing my fingers against hers in a series of premeditated accidents. "Did you know it only takes eight pounds of force to remove a human ear?"

After the words leave my mouth I wish for a way to scoop them back up and try again. But, surprisingly she smiles, says, "no," then brings the ear to her eye, squints, and tells me to hold still. "Almost fits," she says. Giggling. Mouth open. Her bra strap sliding from her shoulder.

"What?"

"It almost fits where yours is missing," she says and hands the treasure back to me.

"Mine was a torch accident."

And before I can elaborate this woman feeds me shots of black label Southern Comfort— one of my personal favorites—from a flask I would have never found on my own. She then drops down, has me in her mouth with my pants down to my knees and the radio turned up loud enough to vibrate dust. Drunks swagger by the truck, a few stopping for full minutes trying desperately to part the fog. A few holler slurred words, and I'd tell them to fuck off if I thought at all it would rev this woman. I know nothing about her other than the feel of her cracked red lips.

Numbers pass on the LED clock, two minutes, five minutes, ten minutes, and still I'm enjoying every move this woman makes. I return gestures where I can, hindered and sloppy, and she seems to like it, but what do I really know about pleasing this woman? Just as I finish she is asleep and snoring to the beat of the music all around us. I wad my pants under my head and bury myself in the heat of our sweat.

I wake up with one of her hands pulling from my pocket and one holding a piece of paper close to her face. Her cracked lips dance as she reads. "What's that?" I ask. She doesn't answer. I move her hand out of my pocket and feel for my wallet. Satisfied I ask again about the paper.

"How long have you been gone?" she asks with genuine compassion.

"A few hours, I guess," and I look to the dashboard clock to confirm. "Yeah."

"From home, I mean."

Home. She says it, rounding the "o" until her lips collapse upon themselves to finish the "m-e." I don't understand his woman's motivation, but I go with it anyway. "After my father died, my mother and I simply drifted. I've been bouncing from friend to distant relative to stranger's couch for the last twelve or so years. I have what my uncle calls, nomadic roots."

"Those don't sound like roots at all."

"Okay."

"Did you ever stay with your uncle? When you were homeless?"

"My uncle is fucking crazy."

"Crazier than a boy trying to get along without a mother? Without a family at all?"

The woman lifts a dirty coat from the floor and pulls it tight around her, lowering the radio volume on her way back to her seat. The change makes my head throb. I'm considering her question, but she asks another. "She loved you, though?"

She loved me? What we had was a relationship based not on affection, admiration, or *love*, but one based on sidestepping those very qualities in order to secure a communal, rather than familial, house. Tension claimed crevices like mold.

My first word was cunt and by the age of five I spoke only in dick jokes. My father was good to me when he was alive. He taught me how to love a woman, using a pillow. But in effort to attune this woman to my sensitive side, a side I still care about producing even after getting off, I pretend to think hard about my past and say, "well, she always made big meals for me."

She smiles. "You ever going back?"

I scan her body, remembering the way if fit against mine. "Sure."

"When?"

"Why?"

"You should," she says and closes her eyes, settling back into the dusty passenger seat. Before shutting down she sets the paper on the dashboard and repositions a heat vent behind her head. I watch the paper ride a stream of hot vent air. "Wait, wait," I say and shake the woman awake. "This isn't my mom."

The paper is the Kevin Masons ad from my back pocket. I laugh to curb any embarrassment and shake my head softly while I gather the right words. "I just wanted to show this to people. It's fucking crazy isn't it?"

She looks to the paper.

"This isn't from my mom. My name isn't Kevin Masons. I found this thing in the paper yesterday. What do you make of it?" I press the paper against the windshield and iron it free of creases by the heat of the sun and my palms.

"You took away that woman's only chance to be happy," she says, grabs the paper and crushes it in a single gesture. *"You're* fucking crazy." She digs through the trash and clutter of my truck for what I realize too late is the rest of her clothes. By the time she has them she's made up her mind to leave.

She opens the door to a cool breeze. Her smell escapes. Unsure what comes next I try to fill my future with this woman, placing her at Thanksgiving dinner, Christmas morning, the Fourth of July barbeques but can't succeed, and she is stretching the distance between us so quickly. Wanting to keep the option to make up my mind later I yell before she is too far gone, "can I get your number?"

She turns, seems to want so much to yell, to smash every rusted hinge of this vehicle, but she settles and pulls a pen from her pocket. She writes few quick numbers in the gutter of the Kevin Masons clipping, wads it again, and throws it into the truck. "Here," and she is gone again, her thighs kissing with angry speed.

⊞

Driving home wasn't like driving at all. It was like riding with zero control. I knew something had to have happened between memories but couldn't stitch the time together with the travel I knew must have existed. I remember a few horns and a few red lights but nothing else. I think her name was Tammy.

But Tammy was right and she deserves to know it. I'm stopped at a dead gas station with a heavy black phone in my hand, reach into my pockets for some change but find them empty. She wiped me out, leaving me with only the ad and a copy of her bar tab. Without any money I head home to make the phone call.

FIVE

I Know Kevin's Mother

An *-er* job pays enough for a small studio apartment, electricity, some water, and a live phone line which is really all that matters by the time I reach my front door. I've neglected all else, trailing mud from shoes I refused to remove; my jacket remains buttoned, and the door, I leave it unlocked behind me where normally I would have shut it, locked it, and bolted it before the airs could mingle. I think I want to apologize to Tammy.

Even drunk I realize that what I'm doing promises no positive outcome. I ruffle through my pocket anyway, grabbing a random piece of paper, and end up dialing Town Royale's address twice before realizing I'd grabbed the bartab instead of the paper with the woman's phone number. What did Tammy look like, I tried to remember, but ignore the details because all I need to know is that she needs to be on the other end of the phone. I yell at the recording as it patronizes me for a misdialed number. I hang up, curses all the way down.

I finally call Tammy's number, finding it buried in my pocket, breathe deep. I've memorized what to say. I'll start with "Hey," and ride what comes next, eventually gearing the conversation toward an apology. Unless, she's hostile. In that case she doesn't deserve an apology. She *did* order an expensive beer, and she *did* steal my wallet, but then again, she *did* fit so well in my lap. I lay down on my dirty carpet to stop the world from moving. The phone rings and rings and rings and ri...

"Hello."

"Hey," I say and wait for the flow.

"Who is this?"

She sounds different. "I miss you already," I say.

She's dead for a few moments. Like hours. Then, somewhere out of the silence she asks, "Is this ..."

"Yes. I just wanted to say"—a deep breath—"that I'm sorry."

"No," she says. "I'm—"

"No. It was my fault. I shouldn't have said all that crap. I was drunk and you were nothing but good to me. I wish I would have realized this earlier but I didn't—"

"You don't have to—"

"I realize it now though, and I want to say I'm sorry. I want you to know that... Look, I want to see you again."

She's dead again. I can hear a TV in the background roaring with game show applause. The bag over my broken window flaps and flaps and fl...

"Why don't you come home," she finally says. "We miss you."

Somewhere within those words I've vomited all over my chest.

That goddamn bag. Flapping. Flap, flap.

"We had the police looking for months. They stopped and told us to expect the worst—"

Somebody yells from the background.

"—but we wouldn't stop."

Wiping the mess from my face with the tail of my shirt I try to remember the beginning of this conversation, the genesis of our misunderstanding but nothing fits. I'd hang up the phone if the receiver were closer.

"You must've found the ad," she says.

"Tammy?" Bile burns my gums.

"Come home," she says. "Come home. Come home..." sobbing loud enough to hide the applause now muffled in the background.

"Wrong number," I yell and as quickly as the words erupt I find myself hovering over the telephone receiver. I set it down and say "sorry," long after the line is dead.

Wanting to try again I take the Kevin Masons ad from my pocket and look to the reverse side for Tammy's correct phone number. Backed by the light of a shadeless lamp I see both sides of the paper, both phone numbers—both the same. Fuck Tammy.

The night can't die. I want it to but the way the world spins, so angry with me, I can't find the calm before the sleep. The vomit dries beneath my head, stitches my hair to the carpet. For fear of a scalping I stay down. The only thing within reach is the telephone and lamp.

I hit redial.

"Sorry," I say when the woman answers. "You didn't sound like my mother."

She cries, and by this time the man's voice behind her has adopted questioning my health in lieu of my identity. "I'm just glad you have a memory of my voice at all," she says.

The silence between us, not even mechanized breath, is too depressing for rebuttal.

She sounds soft, softer than a mother of a runaway should sound. I've already made up my mind that if I were Kevin Masons I never would have left. She seems to truly miss me...to miss Kevin.

"I just had to leave," I say and hope it's what Kevin would say.

"I know. Your father and I both know. What happened should never have happened."

"Yeah," I say. "But at least it can never happen again, right?"

"We don't want it to. I promise you that. Just come home Kevin, please."

Trust: I've gained a bit and given some away, and by now—the vomit hardening on my head, the sun rising breaking the window pane—it probably doesn't matter. She doesn't care about Jackson and his lies. But me, I just want to believe that I recognize the sincerity of a mother's voice.

"I can't be sure, yet," I say and bury myself into this role of defiance. Playing Kevin Masons I say, "You just hurt me so bad. I don't know how I could ever come back from that."

Her tears tighten to gentle sobs. "Wait," she says and goes silent for a moment. She comes back, apologizes for the interruption. "That was your father," she says.

I nod on my side of the conversation like I've known all my life how difficult the man can be. "That's dad."

"He," she says swallowing tears, "thinks you should come home too."

"Really?"

"Of course, you know that."

I find it funny, even though I understand that nothing about this situation *should* be humorous, that no matter how much this woman cries and pretends to understand Kevin's dilemma she is still the one who compromised legibility for cost with her want ad. I open the ad and reference specific sections as I tell this woman all about her lies. I swallow before speaking. "It took me three tries to read what you wrote. I almost passed it up."

"You know we can't buy much these days."

"You could have splurged for the vowels on *please.*"

"We had a lot of newspapers—"

"The world spins. "Did you know that I slept in ditches for the first week? Once out that door I was lost. I didn't know where anyone lived. A kid shouldn't have a street lamp for a night light," and feeling empowered, drunk, and stronger than two rounds of vomit would imply I hang up and drag myself to the bathroom. I'm too late. My chest, my pants, all the carpet behind me stinks of hot bile. But the linoleum floor feels cold against my face and the sensation is enough to make me smile.

Eventually, I hear a dial tone.

SIX

And I Know Uncle Marve

Enlisting Uncle Marve was the country's biggest mistake since starting the war. So says Uncle Marve. He also says that for years after the war all knowledge was supposed to be held in accordance to a strict confidentiality agreement he signed when, as he has said, "They had us signing blank forms, just filled out the fine print later."

I wave to Uncle Marve from across the park. He's got a face like Bat Boy, nothing but teeth and angles.

He's told me of prison camps, inhumane conditions, foreign girls, machine guns, how hot a spent bullet casing gets and shows me the scar he made with one, what MREs taste like, what foreign girls taste like, how to disable a tank, where to go to get clean clothes in a war zone, how to get paid fixing broken tanks, that middle eastern countries have laws against liquor, that all they need is some booze to calm them down, how to hold a rifle, how to load a rifle, and once he explained to me how to make sunglasses out of tree bark, but I forget how.

For breakfast I visit this uncle, my father's brother, whom my father has told me often to leave alone. The man has problems, this much is obvious, but I've never accepted his issues as being reason enough to avoid him. War and whiskey have warped the man's mind to little more than fumes and unstable synaptic clefts, true, but he's capable of humor—the litmus test of sanity. The first time I caught Marve on this bench I told him that I'd amputate this leg if he thought it would help him fit the torn veteran cliché better. We've always been on fine terms. As a kid, he was my go-to vent for all domestic frustration; he never liked my mother either.

Today, he's sitting on his park bench as usual, overlooking a pond that was installed last year as part of Veranda's attempt to bring about communal cohesion. I don't think it has worked; I've never seen blacks or Asians and any others together anywhere near the pond. I drop next to Marve and follow his gaze toward the water. I ask him if he's seen any black people around it lately.

"It's filled with dead bodies," he says.

"So, yes," I say, smiling, just the sort of racist humor Marve appreciates.

He doesn't smile back. "That cemetery at the top of the hill," and he points to a crowd of tombstones that resemble the notches of a castle parapet. "When it rains the water drains right down to this pond. It sits for a while as shallow puddles in collapsed graves, soaks into the earth, then gravity does its thing."

Along with thin, decrepit, crazy, and angry, *morbid* is a top word pertinent to Marve's all-around character. It was him who taught me about the human appendages trade. "I've swam in that water, Marve."

"Nothing wrong with that. There's only something wrong if you do it again."

I hand Marve this morning's breakfast, a sausage and biscuit sandwich from the greasy spoon just up the road on Walmath and Fourteenth. He accepts the bag with a rare smile and slides over for me. "Kid," he says opening the bag. "You're the only reason I stay around."

"There's got to be another one," I say and take a bite out of my own meal, a house specialty—biscuit and gravy sandwich with bacon bits and a spot of paprika on top like confetti.

"Nope." And that's all he gives me.

Most of the general public stay far away from Uncle Marve. Though friendly, his appearance implies otherwise. Uncle Marve looks street-worthy; the dirt, the thin clothes, the unkempt hair, all of this screams homelessness. But Uncle Marve not only has a home—a large one, actually—and a job, but a wife as well. A terminally ill skeleton named Elliot. Homelessness is a hobby. He has limits, though.

"Shitting in trenches and wiping with the sleeve of a nearby dead body is something I've given up since the military. If I found a dead body on the street, I wouldn't even *consider* wiping my ass with it." He's said this with a strange amount of pride, as though it takes true will power to avoid such behavior after having been shaped by necessities during a war.

He's got a metal detector leaned against his thigh and a large canvas bag secured around his wrist by a thin rope. The ground in front of us is dug up in places so I ask him, "found anything good today?"

"I'm not looking," he says.

"Why's your stuff out, then?"

He looks to his lap like the load suddenly appeared and says, "in case I happen upon something that should be mine."

The air is nice and activity abounds in the park— a squirrel missteps on the lone power line across the field and drops hard to the earth—but more dependable than fresh air and accident prone rodents is the desperate hum of Uncle Marve's metal detector. The air may stop and animals may heed caution, but for as long as I've known Marve, the metal detector rarely stops. "How are you going to find it if you aren't looking?"

"Did I tell you Elliot died?" he says, not answering my question.

"No, nobody told me," and I ask how long ago. To the rest of us, Elliot has been dead for years. She's been so sick and reclusive that most people simply assumed the worst long ago.

"Tuesday," he says tightening his grip on the canvas bag.

He covers my hand with his own and says that the only thing he loved more than her was seeing her face when he gave her a long buried treasure. "Everything I found out here, I gave to her."

Throughout our time Uncle Marve has found rings, coins, discarded soda cans, even batteries. He was most happy finding jewelry—obvious why—but found considerable happiness with military shrapnel. Not just the bullets, but casings, rusted gun barrels, and tiny pieces of metal made him happier than even the events which brought about these relics might have made suicidal soldiers and angry wives.

I sound off a short list of his findings, including the soda cans and batteries, saying "even those things?"

"Everything."

"She wanted all that trash?"

"Nope."

"Who gets that stuff now?" I ask.

He pauses for three deep breaths, says, "someone," and stands slow enough for me to feel the cracking of his bones vibrate through the bench. He walks to the empty park in front of us and kneels down between two turned black patches of dirt. He pulls a small spade from his canvas bag and digs.

Uncle Marve loved war. I don't remember which one he fought, though he's told me many times. Initially drafted as a radio specialist he was eventually demoted to stacking bodies, as the need for body transport slowly started outweighing the need for communication ("sounds like a domestic issue to me," I joked). While there he met a man named Yossarian who would go on to fill Marve's stories for life. According to Uncle Marve, Yossarian was a "clandestine combatant for the true fight," a "hero to all those who wanted nothing to do with immorality," a "thorn so thick he plugged his own hole." When a medic brought Yossarian's dead body to the shed he told Uncle Marve of all the great things the man had done. A favorite of both mine and Uncle Marve's was his "heavy editing" of letters to be sent to the families of the soldiers. Yossarian would leave only the name and the salutation.

Uncle Marve continued these clandestine traditions by not only editing letters himself but also by stitching pockets shut, forging personal letters from the U.S, and singing the "Star Spangled Banner" in made-up German. This latter act, he claims, ultimately led to his discharge, a reaction he insists was ridiculous. "But I got out," he had said, "as far as anyone really can get."

"You're my Yossarian," I tell him. "My Gatsby."

He smiles. "I never met Yossarian. I only heard

about him."

"And someone you've never known will know you. I promise."

Kneeling down in front of the turned dirt he begins dumping the canvas bag full of found metal into the holes. "Just like shitting in a trench," he says. "Leaving behind crap nobody wants but knowing that someone, somewhere down the line will have to deal with it." He laughs a little before coughing, spitting, resting for a few moments, digs again.

"How long have you been burying stuff here?"

"Just since she died," he says with a heavy wheeze.

"How'd she die?" I ask and immediately regret the question considering her sickness.

He drops a fistful of metal into the ground, covers the hole, and moves onto the next. "Luck, I guess."

I let this comment drift. I once provoked an explanation after an equally cryptic claim of a conspiracy involving the Kleenex Corporation's plan to keep noses irritated. He revealed his theory: "You ever notice all that dust that fills the air when you rip one of those tissues from the box?", then without a single hesitant move, kicked me in the shins and told me not to worry about reasons anymore.

"You must've really liked seeing her happy," I say, "to give her everything you found."

"I just liked giving." He digs again into the dirt, and drops in a handful of coins and few metal hair barrettes. "And people like getting."

I kneel down beside him. "And if they find it themselves," I say, "all the more inspiring."

He shakes his head. "I don't care if anybody finds this crap. Sometimes you've just got to know something is out there. Even if you don't take it, you've got to have something to wonder about. We've got time and a brain—might as well use them." He fills the hole with dirt, moves on to the next. From above, the turned dirt is a strange shaped hole, a human-sized letter "t," serifs and all.

"That's enough," he says standing next to me, brushing dirt from his pants. He hobbles back to the bench. "She was great. Never liked her the way I thought a husband should like his wife, though. We had our own style of affection."

"Didn't you love her?"

He shrugs. "I suppose, but it was different than what most people think of as love."

"What now?"

He shakes his bag above the earth. "I cashed in on a pretty good life insurance policy. I have a whole house full of stuff I can sell. A lot of her family are pretty good people. And she had good enough taste in furniture. I'm taken care of." A tiny fragment of some rusted gun stock, a bullet maybe, falls from the bag.

"You never told me Marve, do I have any Marve-shaped cousins out there?"

"I fell from a tree when I was about your age. A branch split me right up to my sack. That tore me up enough to ensure I never had kids. Absolutely true."

I match his smile. "A good pair like you and Elliot never gets any kids and someone like my mother is allowed to spit me out. That doesn't seem right."

"She gave birth to you Jackson, but she's not your fucking mother. Forget her."

"I want to."

"It's about reciprocity. The mother needs the kid, the kid needs the mother. Take out the 'need' from either pair and you've got either a woman who considers her son an obstacle, like in your case, or you've got a boy who is just floating around without roots."

"Or you've got both," I whisper.

"Or you got both, yes."

I stir those words in my head for a few beats, weighing the possible cost of revealing the Kevin Masons ad to Uncle Marve. "Hey Marve, what would you say if I told you about this situation I'm in? A mother situation?"

"Why now?"

"What?"

"It's been years since the car accident. Why finally talk about it?"

"What car accident?"

He sighs, disappointment it seems motivating the exhale. "It's hard to trust a man," he says, "who refuses to free a few secrets."

Then quick, without another word Uncle Marve stands from the bench, pats my shoulder, and limps away. I'll come back in a few days, as I always do, and he'll be waiting on this bench, as he always is. It's good to have family I can count on.

When I get home I dial Kevin Masons' mother, charity and a smile prepping my voice, and find artificial sadness just in time before the woman answers with a perky "Hello."

"Sorry...mom." And she starts crying.

SEVEN

Beating Creg

After filling four vending machines at the local high school, three machines inside a small office complex on the West End, and a few smaller machines at the bus station, I make my way to Luisa's Laundry with the Kevin Masons ad tight in my fist.

Creg scribbles, watching a commercial for fruit nectar. The noise of the bell above the door bothers him—he grunts—but not enough to pull him from the TV screen and his notebook.

The laundry is empty today. Fridays are never a particularly busy time, but even considering the imminent weekend and present day jobs a Friday morning might still manage to bring a few families, a few men emptying shopping carts, a few lonely citizens with a single dirty shirt and an afternoon to waste. Today, though, the entire place is calm, lacking the heavy rumble of dryers, the off-balance washing machines, and the children brought to fists over a few stray coins for a snack or a round of videogames.

I unfold my fist, say "I beat you, man," and flick the balled paper to his chest. He opens the ad slowly, and I give him a few moments to piece together the words considering the frugality of consonants. "I called her," I tell him. "She thinks I'm Kevin. I fucking won. I found my mom first."

He studies the ad for longer than I'd hoped he would before handing it back. "It wasn't a race," he says, retreats to the TV. "And that's not your mother."

"True and true—"

"And you've always said you didn't want a mother."

"True, but—" Luisa steps out from behind her counter, gives Creg a sheet of paper. He nods, receives her strong hug, and folds the paper small enough for his pocket.

"Disrespectful secrecy. I showed you my note," I say.

He pulls out his paper, balls it up, throws it at my chest. An address, a few scribbled notes. Just an *errand* for Luisa. "Why?" he asks. "You know you've taken that woman away from her son."

"She took herself away," I say. "I'm giving her the chance to come back."

Creg writes something in his notebook. "All for her," he says. "Right. I don't believe that."

"Don't give me your trip," I say. "I've already been

robbed by a prostitute because of this note. I don't need you, too."

He doesn't even challenge the claim. Maybe he can smell her perfume still buried in my pores. I can. Or maybe he knows me enough, knows that I can talk the right words when I need to. He rotates back to the TV and ups the volume.

"Maybe she's a cool lady, you know? Maybe she knows I'm not her son, but she doesn't care. Maybe Kevin was a fuckup all around. A mother should be honored to have me as her son."

"Maybe."

Just over Creg's shoulder on the front of the vending machine, dulled, faded, hangs a poster I placed months ago. Rows of kids with bad haircuts and crooked smiles—smiles because they know where home is, what home means—all hang brandished by these weeks and weeks of sun. Creg hasn't touched it. Motivation, I'd guess. I point out a random computer enhanced image of a three-year old turned nine: "Kevin is more than just a photograph now," I say. "He's a voice. And she seems happy with it."

"You're the caring son she's always wanted," he says.

"Maybe I am."

Creg rolls his eyes, and sure I'd like to punch him, but rolling eyes I suppose, is what little he can do. I've happened upon this mother; he can't stand it. He can't swallow the fact that I'm part of something now, that I've been accepted and Step Two is a kind letter, Step Three is an envelope full of photographs, Step Four is a reunion with a big meal and stories I can pretend to remember. I grab a Baby Ruth from B-6 and tear the wrapper with my teeth. Creg lights a cigarette. He sets the unpuffed stick in an ashtray and breathes the smoke deep.

"You know," I say, reaching over to a paled image of a forgotten child. "Most parents don't even lose their kids to kidnappers in crowded malls." Creg's writing slows. "They don't even lose them to strangers at amusement parks or whatever the hell TV tells you. Learning this was part of the training when I worked for the Missing Children's Network."

Creg stops his pen completely. "You didn't have to train for that job."

"You'd be surprised how many are actually abandoned, like in gas stations and grocery stores. A lot of times the parents file a report just to keep people off of their backs. They give the police an old picture, one with bad lighting or with a shorter haircut. The parents pretend to cry and they pretend to worry, but the truth is, in the loads of spare time they now have without the kid, they live it up. They buy a boat. They move to Mexico."

"Fuck you, Jackson." He rises, turns the TV louder.

"But sometimes," I say, returning the volume to a

murmur, "Sometimes they really do want to be together. This could be one of those times."

Luisa yells from the back room, something about her finger, and Creg jumps to investigate. I follow until certain he can handle the situation—a gauze wrap and some peroxide suffices to mend whatever small wound she has—then float back to the front and steal a few drags from the burning cigarette. Between puffs I vandalize the dirty pages of his notebook.

By the time he comes back to the TV I've smoked his entire cigarette and filled half a page of his notebook with false descriptions and misleading notes. I write blurbs of fake advice I hope he heeds years from now when going back through these pages, searching for the lead that might have been. I write, *phone calls to executive producer of* Televisión Chistosa *remain unreturned* and *never mind pages three through thirty-six—they were all reruns from before my birth*, and *Jackson rules*, underlined twice. Creg catches me, finds these messages as soon as he returns and blacks them out with deep, heavy strikes.

"Everything okay back there?" I ask.

"Luisa is fine. She steamed her hand pretty bad, though."

After covering most of my marks, cussing under his breath, he finally just rips entire pages free and throws them behind the vending machine. He reaches for his ashen cigarette, a move I interrupt with the first thought that comes to mind. "We should call Kevin's mom right now." His mouth open, he wants to tell me how ridiculous I sound, how repulsed he is by the idea, but he can't. "You'll hear how happy she is," I say. "She deserves us."

"For her?" He asks.

"Of course. For her." I pull him without much resistance to the telephone bolted against the back wall. He feigns defiance but still steps of his own accord.

"But I don't agree with what you're doing," he says.

"*We're* doing," I correct him. The phone is ringing, too late for him to step away.

"Hello." A voice, always perky.

"Mom," I say. I pull Creg to the earpiece, can feel his cheek tighten as he smiles.

"Oh, Kevin. I'm so glad to hear from you again."

Luisa appears, inspecting the gauze as she swallows two pills without water. Creg tries to pull away, but I hold him still. "I just want to make sure none of this is my imagination," I say.

"Of course not," Kevin's mother says.

"How's dad? Is he ready to talk yet?"

"He stepped out. Errands."

Luisa hovers; her shadow encapsulates us, stretched by the sun pouring through the front window. I can hear a game show in the background.

"So," and I wink at Creg, shrug. I don't know what I'm saying, what I should say. "Mom?"

"Yes, Kevin."

"I love you."

Static pads the silence. "I love you too."

Creg attempts pulling away again, but I grab his shirt, a damp tee so worn it's sheer. He whines, and points to the TV, but I hold tight. He whispers that Fridays are *test afternoons*, a term he's used before but never explained.

I whisper: "This is your test afternoon."

"What?" Kevin's mother asks.

"Nothing, mom. Some annoying prick wanting to use the phone."

"Come home, Kevin," she pleads. "Your father and I both want you back."

"Can't," I say and surprised by the insistent invite I reach for the only truth I know. "I hurt a man; I took his ear. If I go back home I'll be found."

"What?" she asks.

Creg fights the phone from my hands, covers the mouthpiece with his own hand, and furrows his brow. I whisper that I'll explain later, pulling the phone back, and when I get the earpiece to my head the mother is mid speech and all I've caught is "... does that mean?"

"It's a long story," I say. "We'll just have to stick with the phone for a while."

"Fucking liar," Creg says loud at the telephone. I

71

push him far enough away to minimize damage but hold his sleeve tight to keep him from running free. This is his intervention, his window. He's fighting my grip, telling me that I'm cruel and that I should hang up right now and that I've got no heart, no decency, and *no right*, he says like he alone has no mother. He still struggles so I kick his legs out from under him and lay across his chest. With his elbow in my rib and one hand in my face he grabs for the phone. This short struggle ends with me again catching the tail end of something that sounds important: "... and grandpa finally died."

"Oh," I say, breathing heavy, biting fingers. "That sucks."

"Everything was pretty painful for him toward the end. Seems we had a tube hooked up to every vein by the time he finally dropped out. Luckily, though, he seemed pretty out of it."

"Cancer will do that," I say.

"Heart attack."

Creg hears this, morphs his anger to laughter. "Right. Right. It's been a while," I say and she agrees.

"They're going to read the will sometime next week," she says, slowing the words as she nears the end until the statement sounds like a question. "It would be great for all of us if you were there."

I've always wanted to be part of a will. In the movies, on TV, the survivors are always blessed with money, mansions, and entire estates. Especially if the deceased is old, as would be the implication here with the grandpa. Creg is spitting in my face now, still laughing.

Hoping to dodge the invitation despite its potential I say, "Didn't he hate me?"

"He hated everyone," she says. I fake a small laugh. Hers, I can tell, is honest.

"I'll have to think—" but from behind us Luisa grabs the phone and slams it down on the receiver. She yells about phone bills and emergency use, but by judge of her anger she's been listening in, waiting until this perfect reason to step in.

"That was Jackson's mom," Creg pleads, but Luisa is already walking away, shaking her head, repeating "no, no, no," like we've crossed a line. And we both know we had, looking at each other with smiles revealing our outed curiosity; we've already seen the other side.

Creg looks to his watch. "I'm going home."

I had planned to fill my evening with the downtown vending machines, but the call with Kevin Masons' mother has me anxious to dodge the day-to-day grind as much as possible. She's a voice. She a direction I didn't know existed and a nagging wind just powerful enough to push me along. Creg is already out the door. I chase after him.

Outside, it doesn't rain on us. But I feel like it should.

"I'll be seeing you," Creg says and begins walking

away.

I offer a ride which he reluctantly accepts on the condition that we can run by O'Malley's on 41st before dropping him off. He pulls out the paper Luisa handed him earlier, says this errand needs to be done today.

"Of course," I say, fueled by the exchanged I love yous.

EIGHT

We Covered This Place with Graffiti

For most of my life I lied about deafness. I would lie to people, again, and on this would go until either I laughed or they gave up on me. Usually the latter. I would explain, like it was still funny after all that time: "See, I was in this accident when I was younger," as the melted ear showcased this obvious fact. I've used this joke on Creg many times so when I throw the dried prune that is Marion Garza's stolen ear at him and say, "two ears now, I can hear just fine again," I'm sure he gets it, but he doesn't laugh. Instead, he leeches hard against the passenger door and swipes at the ear until it falls to the floorboard.

"What the fuck is that?" he says.

I punch him in the knee on my way down to retrieve the relic. Blowing the dirt out of its crevasses, "This is what I was talking about with Kevin's mom."

"What the fuck are you doing with it?"

"I'm going to pawn it," I say.

"Let's just get to O'Malley's," he says wiping his hands on the vinyl seat.

O'Malley's is an upscale laundry sitting just inside the town limits where Veranda becomes the richer Maston. Maston is known for its restaurants, hotels, and live theatre. Veranda is known for being that town connected to Maston. Driving by I would have never noticed O'Malley's, and especially not as a laundromat, if it weren't for Creg's eyes. The O'Malley's sign is almost hidden, scripted in a small monotype font above the front door. We wait until a man with a blue drawstring bag and a set of keys locks the door behind him as he leaves. I park the truck a block away and we walk with our own bags full of faux laundry and spray paint.

"Can't be upset with timing like that," I say.

Creg trips over a curb, catching himself with a stop sign. "You don't have to come," he says.

"Why wouldn't I?" and then casual, like following a lifelong shortcut, we duck into the back alley and unload supplies behind a dumpster, onto which some clever individual named Mike had stated that he *was here*. I gesture to the graffiti.

"Maybe monopolizing the trash industry in exchange for *digital* TV," Creg says. "This neighborhood looks like a digital TV kind of place." He pops open a can of purple spray-paint the cap claims is Fuchsia Sunset.

Artist Creg coats the wall with timid seduction,

leaning in, stepping back, and attacking in impressive bursts of color. The nozzle breathes in Morse code, three short bursts to fill in the shadow of a giant *d*, three long to form the smooth curve of a *y*, and three more short to touch up the outline of an *s*. "Edys," it says, and when I ask he tells me it is a Maston gang he just made up.

"Isn't that ice cream?" I ask.

He steps back and stares, chewing on his purple thumbnail. "Yeah."

My first act as a vandal apprentice is to cover the name *Mike*, with my own name using a Sliced-Lime Green. Next I paint a rainbow on the back wall of O'Malley's, but with only this single shade of green the image doesn't translate well. "Or it's a dangerous fog," I say. "It communicates, 'Do your laundry here and I will suffocate your children.'"

We both laugh.

Creg pulls out a Tamarind Orange and crafts what looks like Japanese characters over the back door, the dumpster, and around the corner to an exposed west side of the building. The escaping aerosol echoes through the alley. The mixing ball rattles inside the can, its ting reverberating between buildings and off of glass windows that business owners have sealed with curtains to block the depravity of an empty alley. The high sun, falling slowly to Creg's back, burns my eyes. "Shouldn't we wait until dark for that wall?" I say. "Anyone can see you."

"Look at these streets."

True, like old west empty, where even the tumbleweeds are hidden, lacking the wind's encouragement. The overspray from Creg's Tamarind Orange billows above O'Malley's like a lonely fire. The air smells like the latex Halloween mask I once stole from a drug store. When asked by the store owner how my parents could be reached, even then I knew to say, "I have no idea."

"What do you have planned?" I ask him while filling in the eyes of a green smiley-face with an evil looking Ketchup Red I found at the bottom of Creg's bag. "For the holiday?"

"John and Brenda are having a Thanksgiving-thing for all their foster kids. It might be cool. I'll stop in for some stuffing or something. You?"

"Nothing." I could lie, but the truth is humbling how I play it with such nonchalance—*nothing*, like it doesn't matter.

"You could come with me. John's not such a bad cook, really."

"Maybe," I say and finish the word *Microsoft* in large bubble-letters like it means something.

"Or you could go to your *mom's* house," he says stretching the "mooooooom' like he's taunting me with a childhood crush.

"I'm playing a part," I insist.

The orange fog rising from Creg's side of the

building dissipates into the clear air. He tosses the empty can aside scaring a cat out from beneath the dumpster. The animal kicks gravel far into the alley as it disappears around a corner. "Fuck," Creg yells, then throws a second can, almost hitting the cat. He yells, "fuck," twice more as the new can—I imagine its name to be Banana Sunset—bounces against the ground and explodes over a stone window sill, coating the neighboring building with a sharp slice of yellow. I laugh louder than I probably should.

"Shut-up," he says. "And you're not playing a part."

I laugh once more to claim the exchange as mine. "I'm just good at it."

Decorating the name of Creg's fake gang with dots of Ketchup Red I say, "They'll be looking for these Edys guys before anyone else. We could get away with anything."

"That's the idea," he says. "Displacing blame."

I indulge in this theory's possibilities by smashing a rock into the small window in the back door, hammering until my palm bruises, until the mesh support gives way for my hand, my forearm, my elbow and at this best moment Creg finally steps around the corner with what I tell myself is the start of an optimistic smile.

Fuck you, it sounds like he says, ducking, scanning the alley for bystanders.

I work the deadbolt free with my wet hand. The

door slides over broken glass, grinding the bits into the ground and our shoes as we step inside.

I smell soap—not the stale curtain of cigarette smoke and disturbed dust like Luisa's Laundry, or any of the others on my route, but agitated soap suds and steam still wet in the air. By the time I find a light switch Creg has already found a TV set and panics because, "they *do* have digital fucking TV," he says. He grabs a remote control and stares. "They've got a whole Spanish lineup. My mother could be huge, and I don't even know it."

With the lights on I clearly see the potential. To bring down a place so close to perfection holds more promise than any streak of Banana Sunset over a dull wall. The alley was fun, but in here the contrast of angst against radiance would mean true perspective. Outside a dab of color comes across as a petty irritant more than claim to the space. But against these brilliant walls—Heaven would look destroyed painted anything other than white. And Creg must agree as he is already shaking a can of Bermudian Wave Blue. He paints quick layers on the TV screen, coughing on the fumes.

I watch him coat the screen, blocking out this ephemeral possibility of his mother. His eyes glaze over; he blames the aerosol fumes. "I can take care of it," I say, still faithful to my Ketchup Red. "Go ahead and take in the digital lineup while you can."

He stops spraying. "A little late," he says trying to

wipe the screen clean with his sleeve. When the sleeve doesn't work he finds a bottle of bleach and pours, choking, too, on those fumes.

My subtle defacement elevates, from random stabs of color on walls and keyholes filled with a jet stream of paint, to a destruction I can't help but read into. It's not that I'm cruel or seeking liberation. It's not that I believe this *isn't* the way everything should go. It's not that I believe the opposite. I'm not punishing the O'Malleys. But I do feel in control—like I've stabbed a caged animal. This is a conscious and satisfying destruction. I throw cans and quarters into spinning dryers, fill steam wands with soda and juice from the vending machine—a causality I don't mind absorbing—and make my way to the small fleet of washers along the far wall.

After tipping the first machine the second is easy, then the third, but the fourth taunts, a washer-dryer combo unit that for me alone sits impossibly heavy. I turn to Creg for help. Along the floor he has painted the words *Channel 64, red hair, entrance from left, 5:36pm*. Without my asking he says, "Well, *you* got any paper?" When I shake my head he offers a fact I hate: "The perpetrators always come back. I'll write it down later."

We push from the left and watch the tower fall, starting delicate, then slam against the hard ground, blocking our entrance. When it hits and we share our sweaty smiles I know that we've, together, adapted already to this new version of normal. One more tower becomes two, becomes three, becomes common until refusing this community would only mean trying to join again later when the family has fractioned and bonds are conscious. *The perpetrators always come back.*

Three more combo units we tip, forgotten laundry spilled to the floor, and both of us are panting like strays, like brothers, happy despite the way we both know we should feel. And this, I believe, is what keeps our sweat pouring for another row, and another—this satisfaction of becoming something we know we shouldn't become.

We're exhausted, and with only the south wall of washers left undamaged, Creg sits atop a fallen machine and asks about my fake relative's will reading. "When she sees you she'll know."

"I'm not actually going," I say and steal two slightly chilled bottles of chocolate milk from the beaten vending machine. I take a four-second gulp of one before giving the other to Creg. "The phone is close enough."

"But what if the uncle left you something nice?" He opens the milk. "Like a car or a house, or something?"

"Grandpa," I correct him and tell him I have a house. I have a car.

"You rent a studio apartment. You drive a company truck."

"Why don't *you* go?" I say, tossing the empty milk bottle behind a fallen row of washing machines. The glass bounces loud, klink-klinks, against the ground. "The way I see it she has only my voice. You can fake a voice."

He sips for a few minutes, almost considering the idea it seems until sirens crescendo in the distance. He grabs the trash can, empties it on the ground, and beats it against the glass door until he's made a hole just large enough to shove his head though without cutting his neck. "They are headed this way," he yells, and both of us scramble for the back door. I pause to take seventeen dollars from the cash register. Creg is too occupied with a fallen machine blocking the door to question me.

Together we are working the back door when two officers kick in the front. Them fighting through the destruction gives Creg and me time enough to slide the fallen machine just enough for our malnourished frames to squeeze through. But as I'm out, pulling on Creg's arm, a dryer explodes by the pressure of a heated can I planted earlier sending Raspberry Cocktail Salmon Red and the dryer door into Creg's face, dropping him to dead weight. The situation forks—*me or him*. I say a silent apology and haul ass to the GreenAmerica truck.

I see Creg's west side mural vibrating in my rearview mirror. What I thought might have been art around that corner is nothing but vandalism, random scratches of color without direction, without structure—all motivation, a simple claim to the space. As the distance grows the paint blurs until it, along with the flashing police lights, vanishes.

NINE

Thinking of Delaware

*T*he lizard changes Marion Garza's gauze three times before finally stopping to change her own. She leaves him with her bottle of Vicodin and says, "I'll be right back," winking with a smile despite her unsteady strut. He sits alone in the artificial warmth of his truck counting the beats in his head. Still, he is dizzy without his ear and wonders how he will explain the missing feature to curious children. He used to tell them how he was a great boxer and when a man becomes a great boxer his ear will mutate like his. Now he has to explain a simple thief.

He has no claim now but his large arms and girth. He isn't well spoken, widely trained, or good for much more than cutting necks and scaring those unaccustomed to the gentility of a giant. While these assets have served him well until this moment he supports now his bleeding head and dismisses out loud that they will be enough to find the cunning thief. "I am nothing," he says and every breath is the truth.

Voices conspire from the CB radio. He would join but what soul from that pool would offer conversation? None. He's never learned to make friends and must settle for only being one. Reaching out isn't something he is equipped to do without his beaten ear, his proof of a life lived and conquered.

The lizard steps out from the poorly lit rest stop bathroom with a handful of hygienically sealed food stuffs, Twinkies, potato chips, candy bars, crackers, and two bottles of milk—all overpriced and rightly so considering the desperation of people this far from any community—and dumps all of it to the seat asking Marion Garza for help as she struggles into the cab.

His rig lumbers out of the parking lot, shaking, hissing and moaning until satisfied by the smooth road underneath. Marion Garza relaxes into the road. He pops another Vicodin.

"Was he a big man?" he asks wiping his lip then tossing the bottle behind him.

"Yeah, I suppose so."

"How tall do you think?"

"Five-eight, five-ten."

"Was he white?"

"He was somethin'."

"And you're sure he's going this way?"

She doesn't answer at first, just exhales a flurry of crushed orange Andy Capp's Fries powder like she's answered the question so many times before—and she has, four times already, followed each time by, "he said the part museum. You know any other part museum?"

And each time he says, "I don't know of any part museum."

But they do exist. And they'll take a cauliflower ear, attach a story stolen from some local legend, and charge tourists five dollars for a postcard.

"Those places don't exist." Through the phone Kevin's mother forces a disbelieving sigh.

"Yes," I say. "They exist. They're dotted all over, but most just carry artifacts, crap some old man found in his backyard when planting azaleas: dog teeth, bird bones, maybe the occasional arrowhead the curator claims killed the local town founder a hundred years ago. Travel two hundred miles out of your way for one of those dumps and you're likely to trash the joint for your wasted time. But this place I know, it takes *contemporary* exhibits, and pays plenty."

"Sure," she says. "But after that why don't you come home? Do your thing then come back home."

"You're not listening," I say:

They have a thief to catch.

These two are close. They *won't give up because* the lizard *won't give up. Marion Garza is a passive man, always has been, and could go on just fine aside from a few alterations in his life story if it weren't for Gina. He couldn't claim boxing anymore, but he could claim war. The more he thought about it the more the idea appealed to him. He could conquer the truth for an even better story.*

"If we find my ear and your foot, then what?" he says gnawing a Chic-O-Stick.

She crushes an empty bag. "We can have our parts back. As long as Jackson doesn't offload them I'm fine with watching them shrivel, just on my own terms."

"I don't want to see that," he says. "What will you do when we find him?"

"We should take something of his."

He agrees and suggests a quick finger or two.

"The whole arm," she offers.

"A sheet of flesh ..." and on and on, tossing ideas like missiles; from stolen parts to stolen limbs, to death, quick death, painful death, full-on torture, and with each shot they get closer and closer until shared goose bumps grind their shoulders. "Paper cuts," she says and "shotgun shells full of rock salt," he adds and "sandpaper—"

"You know all of this?" Kevin's mother says. "Are you with those people right now or something?"

"I don't need to be. I know these people. I know how they think, even what they would say," I wind the telephone cord around my finger. "They're fucking crazy. If they aren't going on like this then they're probably killing purebred puppies or dragging clowns behind their vehicle. People like them, you know they've done some shit and wouldn't hesitate to do some more. I've known Marion Garza for a while. He'll track me down for his ear. I'm a wanted man."

"Such language." she says.

When I first met Marion he approached me with a toothpick in his mouth and asked to borrow a fork from my table. I was planning on using it, but you don't deny a man like Marion Garza anything, especially pointed objects. I knew my place in the trucker's lounge. A small-route delivery truck isn't what the sign means when it says Trucker Seating. *But the guys let it go, even let me bother them with my own stories of the road. My favorite being the time I found an H-200 vending machine fallen on top of guy who, as it turns out, had plenty of change in his front pocket for the purchase of whatever he was trying to steal. The real truckers never let me get to the punch-line—that the man was a diabetic—before cutting me short and boasting about lot lizard conquests and stupid CB call signs. But Marion Garza was quiet, as absorbed in the stories as I was, and after a group of them left he slid over next to me and told me that once, when he worked at a meat packing plant, he stabbed a cow in the eye.*

She waits full seconds. Behind her the TV still blares, the voice of a cardboard game show host pours though with the mother's heavy breath. "You should come home now," she says.

"No. I can't. I've got to move away from my past. They'll find me if I come back."

"They'll find you at the museum," she suggests.

"They'll be waiting."

I ignore her, walk to my kitchen where I keep a stack of state maps in a drawer under the silverware.

I unfold a map of Nebraska and one of Missouri and search for isolated dots, possible cities of asylum, random destinations Marion Garza and Gina would never think to check: O'Neil, Albany, Brookfield, Broken Bow, Thedford. Running the list through the phone, each comes back with either a flat silence or a small breath of recognition. Imperial, Red Cloud, Moberly.

"Moberly," she says. "Vanessa lives there."

"Really?" and I cross the town out with a heavy black marker. Solitude. Isolation. Recognition is a worthy goal but only on my own terms. The last thing I need is a fake family member blowing me wide open. Really. I'd hang up right now. Leave the phone and never return, but she needs me.

She needs to hear Kevin's voice. I do this for her.

"What about Mullen?"

"Never heard of it," she says.

I circle the town in pencil.

"Where will you stay?" she asks. "What will you do for money?"

"A job is a job. I'll find one somewhere. Don't worry."

"I can't help it. That's what a mother does. Especially *your* mother."

"Don't," I say and recite a few more names from

the map of Missouri.

"Why won't you come back? I want a real reason this time."

"A real one, huh?" But I don't have one. So after a meditated pause and a strong sigh I tell her, "sure," but despite where *home* is I continue circling towns from neighboring maps. Broken Arrow. Hooker. Imperial. Each town filled with faceless strangers. Maybe it's the late hour, maybe it's the subtle desperation of Kevin's mother breathing through the phone, but after enough town names I feed her some optimism that her son might be willing to let distance heal. "Maybe I'll swing by for the reading."

She explodes in whimpers.

"Where are you guys living now?"

"Still in Delaware," she says. "I've left your room just as you did. It's all the same."

I circle Valentine, Nebraska. Okmulgee, Oklahoma. Sedaka, Missouri. But my eyes move to the east: Peoria, Illinois. Lagansport, Indiana. Elkins, West Virginia. And because I don't want to forget I write the word "Delaware" on the only white paper close by: a torn chuck from a map of Texas.

TEN

Keeping Creg's Notebook

My only duffle bag has a stubborn zipper with a cartoon character I worshipped as a child pasted on the side. I remember Saturday mornings, TV-glued, with a soggy bowl of cereal. I won the bag in second grade for selling peanuts door to door, the most peanuts sold in the entire class. I was envied by my classmates, and all I had to do was stay away from my own home for a few weeks.

I fill the bag with neat stacks of maps. Endless boasting of festivals and landmarks, topography, climate, and hotel coupons makes for a thick map, so care in packing is critical. Destinations? Check. A path? Check.

For a while Creg and I had a trip south together planned. I had talked him into a drive all the way into Mexico under the guise of a proactive search for his mother. The truth: I planned on wasting a few selfish days massacring the Spanish language with drunken señoritas. We made these plans once, eager and ready, but never spoke of them again. Though, I know he never forgot. A person doesn't forget hope like that.

As the promise of the trip wore off Creg upped the output into his notebook, nurturing his twisted understanding of family by full pages a day. He adopted detailed drawings, crossover channels featuring non-Spanish speaking Latinas, and eventually got permission from Luisa to use her copying machine to reprint his mother's disgusting headshot. He'd jot upon these glorified sheets of toilet paper the names of actresses with shared features, circling noted similarities. I realize then that he never took the notebook with him to O'Malley's, hence his notes spray painted on the floor. Save a friend? Check.

Luisa has the TV tuned to the Spanish channel and a fresh ashtray on Creg's usual table when I arrive. She turns fast to the door, relaxes when she discovers me, and goes back to a steaming iron.

"Sorry," I say and ask about Creg.

"He hasn't shown up," she says then eyes me with subtle accusation. I check my devious grin.

"He wants me to pick up his notebook." I can see it peeking out from underneath Luisa's cash register. "He's sick today?"

She shakes her head. "He wouldn't trust his book to you. And he doesn't get sick. Where is he?"

"Home. He's at home and he's very sad because he doesn't have his notes. He keeps saying what a bitch you are for stealing his notebook." She turns back, all anger. "He's sick," I repeat, flinching. "He's delusional. Temperature of one-hundred and five. And of course he doesn't really think you're a bitch."

"He'd call. He's not sick."

The bell above the door rings, and a family parades in with armloads of clothes. The south fleet is theirs again. Again the children fight for first player on Snow Brothers.

"Serious. He's too sick to call," I say.

The father approaches the counter and tosses down a twenty-dollar bill. For the instant both he and Luisa are occupied—him yelling at his children to "cut that shit out," and Luisa erasing a crease from a sleeve on a bright red shirt—I sneak the bill into my pocket.

"Hey, Arnie," Luisa says and opens her register, pulling out a handful of quarters. "How much?"

He looks to the counter, begins to say twenty but cuts it short when he finds the bill missing. "I laid it down right here."

The two exchange quick blame before falling to me. "Maybe it blew off," I say and get immediately down to my knees to help look. I'm crawling, feeling around.

The wife is already dumping armloads of clothing into washing machines when the father yells, "hold it a second," as he feels his pockets in quick taps like he would for lost keys. "Mas money?" he says.

She answers in rapid Spanish, angry, and continues dumping clothes. The children have solved their feud by sharing space on the control panel. The shorter child gets the joystick. The taller gets the buttons. The children pay no attention to the arguing parents, like they've learned to accept those rocky foundations.

I've circled my way around back to the counter meeting the father, panicked nearly to tears. He still pats his pockets, removing receipts, cigarettes, a small change pouch, all of it tossed to the counter. Luisa drums her fingers.

"I found it," I yell. "I found it," and the father breathes deep, reaching for the bill I wave delicately in front of him. "In return I need a favor. I need a notebook she has." The man reaches again for the bill. I pull back. "The notebook."

He turns to Luisa, she is already stacking quarters in short piles of four, and he asks her about the notebook.

"He can't have it," she says. "It's not his."

"I just need my money," he says to me.

"I need the notebook."

"But it's my money."

"It's my notebook."

"... and twenty," Luisa says releasing the last stack of quarters. The man tries to explain this situation to her, this situation she's been a part of since its beginning, but she shrugs, says, "I guess you should get this boy's notebook." I smirk—an egotistical move she interrupts with a swift grab. "Or this twenty will work."

Fuck.

She closes the cash register, thanks the man, and hands him the TV remote control before turning back to the steaming iron.

"Creg's on to something," I say. "He found a copy of an old audition tape. He needs his notes to verify."

"He didn't find anything. He never will."

"He might," I suggest.

"You're smarter than that." She pulls a plastic sheet over the red shirt and moves the entire package to a metal rack behind her. "She's gone."

"So why won't you give me the notebook?"

"She's gone, but *I'm* here."

"You're just leading him on, then. You're giving him all this hope just so you can watch him fall. If you cared about him you wouldn't let him have all this free TV."

"I don't matter. I could kick him out each day and he'd still find another way. He'd go somewhere, maybe somewhere he's not welcome and fall into real trouble. And who else would be willing to wring the laundry market?" She pauses. "Would you?"

"It's your fault he's locked up," I say.

"How do you know this?"

"I was with him."

"And you left?"

"He was trapped," I say. I take a few breaths, listen to the English flow from the TV set atop my vending machine, the father laughing explaining jokes to his Spanish wife, who smiles only to satiate his need for validation. The children beg their parents for more quarters even as their pockets hang heavy with coins. The family unit: a gelatinous blob of pushing, pulling, writhing, compromise, and failure all set in motion by a couple in need of hereditary commiseration. But buried under all of it, deep, a shared smile, a few I love yous, glow brilliant against the otherwise black dirt. I recognize the words only in theory. Why can't it actually work this way? "And I want to make sure he stays away from here."

"Let him have this one thing," Luisa says. "We know better, but that doesn't mean we're better off."

Another customer enters, a large man holding a wicker basket under a single arm. "Hey Luisa," he yells and she waves back, counting more quarters. I step away when he approaches the counter, telling myself what a nice person I am because of it. But I'm driven more by fear, eclipsed by this man's size.

Not ready to give up I walk over to the children and tell them I'll give them a handful of quarters if they create a diversion by throwing a chair through the front glass window. They don't even consider the offer before running to their parents, scared. My slight pleasure in frightening those kids is compromised by my admitting to the pleasure.

The closest DAV thrift shop is three blocks away. An old woman runs the register, the name "Gretchen" written on a cardboard nametag. She has big hair, big thighs, and a big gut, features a casual glance can take in. I do, however, take time for her shoes: pointed and elevated, maybe two inches at the heels. A person doesn't wear something like without accessorizing with pride.

As casually as I can be browsing a DAV, I stop when I get to the register and tell her how fabulous her shoes look.

"Thanks," she says, smiles.

"I'm looking for,"—take it slow, Jackson—"a ski mask. Any color, really."

"It's getting that time," she says and points to a bin at the corner of the store.

I am invincible.

The only one to conceal my entire face, give triangular windows for the eyes and a small slot for the mouth, is a black number with worn threads at the back, evidence of its endured hardships. Placing it on the counter I fake interest in some elastic waistbanded stone washed jeans. "That's all," I say at the counter, thumbing through a wad of cash, folded over to look twice face value—a trick I use often with women nearby. I throw a five dollar bill in front of the woman. She gives back four bills and three quarters. I slide the three quarters back and say, "keep that close." When I wink she giggles. She does.

By kicking in the door to Luisa's Laundry I hit a child in the face, sending him back into the wall and all at once the entire place is on me like I've done something that weak child won't endure all his life anyway. The crying child's brother seems concerned for a moment before noticing my ski mask and yells, "a robber," over and over, jumping, clapping, and laughing with an equal though misplaced enthusiasm I had hoped the entire laundromat would have. I planned on demanding money—not taking it of course—before grabbing the notebook from under Luisa's cash register. Instead the large man with the wicker basket chases me, tipping chairs, and hurdling machines with surprising dexterity. But I'm more so, and after three quick laps and a final diversion created by tossing a handful of quarters at Luisa I grab the notebook and burst through the back door to my truck which I then remember I'd left running the entire time. I'd be lucky to make it to the county line before running out of fuel.

But I've got the notebook. I can be sure Creg doesn't hold strong to his romantic ideas of a mother. She is just a woman out there with a forgotten child. He is a child reaching out for proof where, I'm sorry to say this Creg, there isn't any. She is fleeting. A mother is an illusion, like poorly-told story.

I do feel bad about taking the GreenAmerica truck. I do feel bad about leaving Creg wherever he is. I do feel bad about leaving Luisa to explain the notebook's disappearance to Creg when he inevitably returns, but maybe feeling bad isn't so bad.

I'm never coming back. Goodbye Veranda. I'll tell the world I was once here.

ELEVEN

Validating Uncle Marve

Three miles away from Luisa's, a full twenty from the county line, the shitty GreenAmerica truck sputters to a stop. The back wheels die just atop the furthest edge of the park. A gas station designed to look like a medieval castle sits just across the lawn so I grab a gas can and walk.

"Hey, boy," a voice yells. I turn to see Uncle Marve sitting at his bench. He's got his metal detector and his canvas bag on full display. "Out of gas?" Those Bat Boy ears of his turn his silhouette angry and fierce.

I walk over and have a seat, stepping over fresh mounds of turned black dirt to get there. "It's a little late for you, isn't it?"

"It's been late for me for years," he says, tosses popcorn from his breast pocket to a squirrel. The squirrel, without investigating, runs up a tree. "Going somewhere?"

"Somewhere's right. Don't know where yet."

"Paris," he says. "Don't go to Paris. Too much pollution in Paris. Go out to the deserts. That's where you have to go for clean air."

"A desert sounds fine," I tell him. "I was thinking about staying a bit closer, though."

"Why?" he asks, sounding almost sincere, though he keeps a strong façade otherwise.

"Maybe to find somebody," I reply.

"Not your goddamn mother, I hope."

"No," I say, quick.

"You talk too much about her. You're one of the lucky ones who got away from the whole family thing before it had a chance to bring you down."

"I don't talk that much about her."

"Look at me. I've seen most of the people I care about fall, one at a time. By the time I get my tears wiped away another body drops down to start the whole process over again. I've spent most of my adult life in the checkout lane waiting to pay for Kleenex. And once you buy a box, you've got to keep buying more. "

"You've told me."

Marve tosses another kernel of popcorn to a scared squirrel. "She wanted to abort you. Your father wouldn't let her. He asked me what I thought about the idea, though. You know what I said?"

I shake my head.

"I gave him my blessing." He shakes a few kernels of popcorn in his fist, trying to entice his squirrel.

"You wanted me dead?"

"I didn't know you. What I wanted was to keep that woman from having a child."

...to keep that woman from having a child... I fight to shake away that phrase as a mantra.

He offers me some popcorn. I accept but quickly let the kernels fall to the ground. Marve seems to have deteriorated substantially within the past 24 hours. His skin hangs translucent over thick, navy veins and his eyes have sunken into his cheeks. I'd accuse him of being high but a man like Uncle Marve would damage a drug.

"I've made it alright on my own," I say, defensive. "I'm not addicted to anything. I don't have a family to support. There're guys worse off than I am."

"You've done alright. Don't go and ruin that by trying to force an element that doesn't belong, okay?" The canvas bag on the ground slumps against his foot.

"Why so cryptic all the time, Marve?"

"Just wanting to approach your history with caution, is all. I'm ready to talk when you are."

...to keep that woman from having a child...

"Find anything today?" I ask, hoping a change in subject may steer us forever away from this tired conversation.

"Not looking," he says, staring somewhere beyond the park.

I match his eyes, try to find his focus in the

distance. Beyond the cemetery pond, beyond his mounds of dirt, I can see only the gas station and a few people toting large shopping bags.

He points to the pond. "Dead bodies in that pond."

"Yeah," I say. "You told me."

"I used to shit in ditches and wipe my ass with my dead buddy's sleeve," he says.

"You told me," I say and change the subject again. "How much more do you have to bury?"

He lifts the bag, tilts his head in thought. "Maybe ten pounds. Not long to go."

"Then what. After you've buried everything."

"Then people find everything. And if those folks aren't selfish bastards the whole thing plays out again."

"You're a good man Uncle Marve," I squeeze his shoulder once before standing, saying, "got to get going. I'll look into your desert idea."

"Not Paris, remember. Polluted air and I knew a scam around there once. They'd take people's money, promise them a condo and great food—all the works—then when they had their heads down to sign the paper they knock the poor souls out, tie them to trees, and take turns raping the shit out of 'em. I know. I was there."

I hide a grin. "Which side were you on, Marve?"

"The backside."

I leave Marve as he stands and staggers his way

to the holes, the canvas bag bouncing against his thigh. When I return from the gas station he has vanished. His empty bag lounges over the bench like a canvas version of the man himself.

TWELVE

Offloading the Ear for Gas Money

O fficially called the Quick Stop 66 and World of Human Oddities—created as such when the once-separate establishments decided it would be worth their efforts financially to combine the two destinations, rest stop and tourist trap respectively, into one—the parts museum creeps onto the horizon outside Veranda, then hits quick, like a materialized roadway mirage.

Its notoriety has served Veranda well despite the occasional citizen's condemnation, those bored folks claiming the place is a "vile and disgusting attempt at shock" and "should not be encouraged, for the sake of our children and our children's children." Once a week or so the *Veranda View* prints a letter from a concerned citizen calling to organize a boycott. My quote comes from Sheryl Lamar, a school teacher and mother. But nobody will shut the place down, claiming the owner's right to business while hiding a general morbid fascination and pride associated with having such an intriguing place attached to their community. Every mayor for as long as I've been conscious has defended the place. Every citizen loves their single degree of separation whether they admit to it or not. Even Sheryl Lamar would have one less thing to bitch about without it.

It is possible to live in Veranda for an entire lifetime without visiting the part museum but highly unlikely that one wouldn't have entertained the desire. Me, I've never actually been, but I know more than a few people who have, and each one calls the experience life changing. Like marriage or parenthood, I've heard. Now, ready to unload Marion Garza's ear, I finally have my reason for the pilgrimage.

I've avoided the place for this long not out of principle or promotion of some strong held belief, spiritual, moral, or otherwise, but because what else would I have to wonder about? Once through those doors I no longer have speculation or curiosity. I have a tactile reference—satisfied or disappointed— and either outcome destroys the endless possibilities I've imagined over the years. In the past I could've wondered how the parts were accumulated or how much they pay, but today I won't even have that.

I walk into the museum with the old watch box stuffed in my pocket, hidden away like contraband ready to be offloaded. The bell above rings, forever it seems. I fit my way into a path around the outside perimeter, a tourist searching for satisfaction. I inhale calm and exhale anxiety. I am normal. *Normal. Normal.* I make it a mantra.

Tiny booths line every wall. I call for an attendant, yell, "I'm here to buy a ticket," but nobody comes. "I've got some merchandise," I call next, but still I'm alone in the center of all these tiny trophies. From somewhere a local radio station softly claims the air, country music backed by the static of contemporary pop. The entire building smells like gasoline and antifreeze, with a formaldehyde aftertaste. Honestly, the absence of flies in a place like this confuses me.

The air itself glows. Multicolored Christmas lights line the wall frieze, each illuminating a tiny, translucent halo of refracted dust and dirt. The air feels damp, the wooden walls swollen with humidity. Misaligned wall planks seem to bloat and wheeze to the measure of my own heartbeat. Jars and wired appendages glow within cranny recesses along the perimeter. This place will map my nightmares for years.

Uncle Marve often told me about this place, each time the topic of my missing ear came up, and every time he'd chuckle when suggesting it might have found its way here. I repeat every time that the thing was burned off, melted to nothing, but I take no offense. Let an old man believe his stories, I say.

He would tell me about the first time he came here, as a boy with his neighbor and her children, after school one afternoon. The place stuck with him, not because of all the human body parts, exactly, but because, he would later learn, "the medium seemed so forced." Having studied three-dimensional design and poetry in the military Uncle Marve was able to look back at his first experience and realize something so odd about the human part museum. His most vehement argument dealt with the curator's apparent desire to exploit the medium without a clear idea as to what it might best translate. To him sculpture—as he claimed these body parts were—was a fine art indeed, but one only to be studied should the idea supporting it be best represented by the form. For instance, if I wanted to express my belief that horse racing owes its success solely to the fact that horse jockeys are a politically correct way for the public to enjoy midgets—should I believe such a thing—I would first decide which form might best suit this idea before bringing it to life in the physical world. A poem, an essay, a charcoal drawing, a novel, architecture, or any one of the endless other options available to best explain my feelings are all to be considered. "The true artist," Uncle Marve said, "knows exactly which medium to use regardless of whether or not he knows how to use it." Later he would admit, "well, I suppose sculpture *was* probably the way to go."

Though, I am still hesitant to call this sculpture. The pieces seem to me more like simple displays.

Documentation, really. Tiny dioramas into a world the tourist might otherwise never know. Maybe the disaffecting simplicity adds to the horror.

These booths contain small pieces collected in effort to have a claim in this gigantic world of ours, a way to fill a mind and a reason to frame the ticket stub. That's what people say, that human parts museums are something so rare you become a part of their legend just having seen one.

I yell again for an attendant, but still nobody comes. So I take a few steps in and start a circle, beginning at the nearest booth. Inset into this closest wall is a small wooden box with a single bulb throwing harsh light hanging from the top. The placard says *Blue Bouquet* with a handwritten description below:

> *After so much begging from his girlfriend, Miguel Marquez set out one night to collect blue eyeballs from foreign travelers to create an eyeball bouquet. He searched in towns and villages close to his own small hometown twenty miles outside Mexico City. After many unsuccessful attempts Miguel finally came upon a small group of students from the United States, from which he took every eye without killing a*

single person. Miguel Marquez was arrested three weeks later while vacationing with his girlfriend in southern Texas.

On loan from an anonymous collection

Without the description I would have assumed the relic to be a collection of grapes glued to wheat straws. But close enough to smell the mothballs I can see the pupils, pruning at the edges like dark, negative raisins. Behind me a mother and child walk into the museum, holding hands, holding cameras. The child appears already pushed to tears, scared as a child should be standing in the same room as severed human body parts and a man with one melted ear and another in his pocket. The mother and I, our eyes meet briefly. I grin. She pulls her child close. Further down the wall, inset into a similar wooden relief shadow box hangs a leg from a yellow thread. *Mysterious Leg*:

Surviving multiple winters without preservation, this dismembered leg finds its way to us still full of holes after having been shot off during a routine hunting expedition. The former owner claimed she remained conscious during the entire ordeal and prayed for a miraculous

recovery. Instead, she says, she was
forced to hobble around on a wooden
leg until even that one was taken,
this time by a traveling Bible
salesman. If you look closely enough
you can see some buckshot still
embedded in the skin.
Donated by a Ms. Hopewell

If I had a camera I'd steal a picture of this one. The knee more closely resembles an infected elbow, shriveled and dotted by a sparse hair. *Ms. Hopewell*, I read again. I wonder who she is without this leg. The next booth, more of a shelf, supports a large glass jar backlit by an eerie green glow, the way a horror movie might strive for fright. What's floating inside means nothing, even after reading the placard, because there's no way in hell I'm staring at a bird tongue. *Tongue of the birds*:

> *"I took only one bite," the donator*
> *said upon delivering this relic,*
> *"before I flew away." Perhaps the*
> *strangest of all the exhibits here at*
> *World of Human Oddities is not even*
> *human. Brought in by a large bird*
> *with a gun, this tongue is said to*
> *have translingual powers, enabling*
> *whoever imbibes the tongue to know*

the language of the birds. After
testing this theory our own station
attendant, Theo Marks, was heard to
chirp before dying instantly of what
doctors later called, "a sudden shock
of insight." He was survived by his
mother and two daughters.

Donated by anonymous bird

I make it a mission to find a postcard advertising this amazing tongue. To whom I would send it doesn't matter. Maybe I'll bless a random address with the treasure. I turn once again to search out an employee, but aside from the mother and her child, the entire building remains empty. By now the two have made their way down the line to the Mysterious Leg. The mother shrieks. The child presses close to the shadowbox glass now, fascinated.

The windowless room seems to darken, like a dimmer switch somewhere slowly putting itself to sleep. I continue pacing the museum, taking in what few words I can still read in the poorer and poorer light.

Inside another jar floats a six-fingered hand the placard says was dropped off by a nameless man who said only that he had suffered enough of people staring. Stapled to the far wall, illuminated by three refrigerator bulbs, hangs a kidney donated by a woman named Jude who stuck around only long enough to wash her hands and collect her small fee. The heart of Mateo Buñoz, donated by a hit-man from his own personal collection, hangs by a string in the far corner.

I'm surrounded by this proof of life, indulging in the final effects of some tragedy or some suffering that has moved beyond the private into the public. Deeper I stare into Mateo's heart, past the object, all the way to the liquid's reflection, me, one-eared me, staring back. The scars on my face ripple in the liquid as a semi-truck pulls into the gas station lot, I can *feel* the engine. The horn sounds, but I'm too engaged to pull away. Every part here belonged to a desperate stranger, someone needing money above all else: money above a complete body, money above a destroyed appendage. Or maybe they needed simple validation, the knowledge that despite a melted ear, or anything else, there are people out there with love on their tongues telling the stories of the felled part and its person, keeping the disfigured alive when the disfigured may be dead to most others: friends, family, dads. And moms. Forgotten elsewhere we are remembered through story. The semi-truck horn sounds again.

A camera flash. I turn to the mother and child. They look away. I feel the space where my ear should be, try to feel for the heat of the flash. Of course I feel no temperature difference, but I do feel the subtle hum of their whispers.

I slide down the display line to a human jaw, title: *Soundbite*:

> *A man arrested by an undercover officer was robbed of his own jaw after his recordings of park birds were found to be of 'lamblike innocence.' This is that jaw.*

But a man with the name Thompson stitched into his greasy grey shirt steps though a heavy red curtain and tells me not to touch.

"Finally," I say and meet the man. "I need to talk to you about something."

He waves me in though the curtain into a common gas station with cigarettes and popcorn and a hotdog rotisserie all thickening the air. By the aid of the new light he takes in my missing ear, breathes deep. "We get everything legally. Don't come looking to offload whatever's left of your head. You can just leave if that's what you're after."

I take out the black ski mask and pull it just far enough over my head to cover where my left ear should be. "It's not like that."

"Because we don't support trafficking. We've got papers for everything on display."

"Not like that," I repeat and reach back into my pocket for the old wooden watch box. "I've come a long way with a great buy. I saw this and though of your place." I show him Marion Garza's ear and his pupils grow by full centimeters.

Then they shrink to slits. "I said we don't do trafficking. That's your ear."

"I found it," I say. "I lost mine in a torch accident. Just look." I pull up the edge of the ski mask to show him my melted leftovers. "I still have my lobe and so does this other ear. Not the same."

Satisfied he offers a shallow grin, apologizes. "I can't help but be skeptical. We get people in here all the time trying to sell off body parts. Nothing big, a finger or two, maybe a sheet of skin, but we can't do it. Legal reasons, you know?"

"Of course. Understandable. But I assure you this is quality. It came from a boxer I knew. He was good, too. Damn good. Then one too many hits to the head and he's out for good. Felt like a waste to let something like this get buried with him." I submit the old wooden box to Thompson. He accepts.

He turns the ear over in his hand, squinting for details, bringing the object up to the light. Three customers enter the store during this time, all three filling their tanks, and all three leaving with a new story about a large man at a gas station examining an amputated ear. I smile to each and make my face as remarkable as possible. They will remember me.

Finally, he throws the ear to the counter—a move I could strangle him for—and says, "This is gum."

"Gum? This is an ear."

"It's gum," he says. "I can see the teeth marks."

I laugh—such a misunderstanding. "See, with a cauliflower ear that happens. The cartilage doesn't get any nutrients and..."

"It's gum. I've seen gum before. It smells like mint."

I drum my fingers on the counter for a few seconds, nervous like I've formulated a deal for this man, a deal that would serve both our interests equally. But because I need time more than money I tell him, "just some gas money, then." I grab three beef sticks from a tub on the counter. "And these."

Thompson runs his hand through his hair and exhales loud. I smell french-fries and tobacco on his breath. "Alright. We've sold bigger lies."

I take offense to the statement: lies? So these oddities are lies? But instead of an angst-fueled fist to his face I give him one last small request: "can I get a ticket stub? To show my friends." Thompson charges me five dollars for the stub, a full twelfth of what he gave me in gas for the ear. He throws in a postcard of the tongue when I beg loud enough.

I exit through the museum, ticket stub in hand. Having been insulted I feel morally obligated to vindicate myself, so I make a show of stepping slowly through the curtain like I cannot be touched.

Slowly I stroll the perimeter again, taking in sights twice, three times, four, wringing every last penny from my ticket. A 24-hour gas station can be a cozy home when home is the empty front seat of a delivery truck.

Nine p.m. by the crooked clock above the curtain and still Thompson hasn't made a move to evict me. Tired, I move towards the exit at the corner of the museum. Just as I step to the cold concrete outside Thompson comes through the curtain with a brown plastic bag and an unopened jug of formaldehyde. He sees me and jumps back, shaking his head once settled.

"Thought you left hours ago. You like this place, huh?"

"It's nice."

"It's been a good day. Just got something new from a couple headed east somewhere." He raises the bag to me. "Since you're still around you want to help with the story copy? You seem like you got some shit in that head of yours."

He disappears into a back room behind what I thought this entire time was a solid wooden wall. He emerges with a giant empty glass jar and some scrap paper. "Think of something real quick. Make it crazy." He tosses a pen from his breast pocket.

"Why?"

"You won't leave." He opens the jar. "Might as well get some use out of you." Pours in the formaldehyde. "My regular guy will be in tomorrow, anyway." Opens the brown bag. "He can give me something better." And the contents ooze out, splash into the jar like shit into a bloody trench.

"Sure." I pop the cap and jot down a few ideas. The best, I think, involves a local legend about neural tissue disease that for some reason affects only suburban upper-class males with two male children. Look close enough and you can see the deteriorated cerebellum, and what looks like the number 666 growing from the frontal lobe.

Thompson looks the sheet over. "Good. Local legends sell. But it's not a brain."

Stepping closer to the jar I ask what it is.

"Looks like road kill to me, but the couple swears it's not."

I flick the glass a few times, pick it up, and hold it to the brightest light in the room—a tiny chandelier outfitted with small, plastic human skulls. When I finally get this better look, backed by the light of the fake bones, I nearly drop the jar. "It looks like a foot to me."

Thompson reaches to take the quivering jar from my failing arms. I pull the jar away. "Can I have my exhibit back," Thompson asks. "And it's a placenta. Not a foot."

"What do you fucking know? That's a foot."

"I know placentas," Thompson yells as the museum door slams shut behind me.

Gina's foot. We had a deal.

THIRTEEN

Selling the Dirty Man's Birthmark

Billboards advertise the famous BETO breakfast buffet for miles turning this small junction in the center of nothing into a destination. Traveling such a long distance, for so long, you allow yourself to be built up too high; you can't be surprised when everything comes crashing down.

Not that the BETO restaurant isn't warming, comforting, and even inviting in a lost-in-the-desert-with-this-last-mirage kind of way, but the road can stretch a person, can leave one strung out on hope, so the truth, when it finally comes, looks more like a lumpy grey soup than an iconic biscuit and gravy platter. I should have gone for the buffet. The buffet is famous, not the menu, but I take my spoon and dive in anyway. A full day on the road without real food is pepper and spice enough to turn this shit gourmet. At this point I'm looking for sustenance a notch above Moon Pies.

Waiting in the truckers' section are two skinny

men and a woman with hair down to her ass. They laugh together, sharing their stories while sipping coffee from engraved souvenir mugs. Slurping the biscuit soup with one hand I grab the telephone at my table with the other. These phones are usually reserved for drivers with credit cards or calling cards—neither of which I have—so I pretend to dial a number and take in the fresh heat from the receiver. Not long ago a driver sat here, spoke here, and if I believed in spirits I might tell the world of a strange feeling in my gut. Two drivers eye me from across the section. When they look I furrow my brow, pretend to hold back tears, like so much bad news is coming through the line. I am a god. I look over to see them staring, hang up the phone, and begin:

This guy I know, Marion Garza, and this lot lizard named Gina I know from a while back, they're close.

At *lot lizard* the woman with living hair and her man slide a bit closer. The dirtier of the two men, a shaggy beard for a face and Western-cut shirt conforming to his body, stays a table away and steals eggs from the forgotten plates. I see ketchup packets and creamer thimbles erupting from his shirt pocket.

These two, Marion and the lizard, started falling for each other—for real falling, not monetarily motivated falling like she's been doing to him for days. And I don't care. She is nothing anymore after keeping the foot money all for herself. There it was, at the part

124

*museum, surrounded by glass with fake story I wrote,
and everyone's five dollar ticket stub will only
contribute to spreading this ignorance. It was her foot.
I'm not stupid.*

*We had this idea together, to go across the country
searching out the most fucked up, twisted specimens of
natural humanity we could, then we'd sell these parts
to the museum back west. It wasn't much money—
money worth doing it for, though—but we were in it
mostly for the name space. Everyone knew about this
place. Every sad truck driver, every disillusioned
vacationing family member, every reader of weekly
supermarket tabloids, they all knew of The World of
Human Oddities. And every one of these people felt it
somewhere deep to commit a few days to a trek in its
name, some sort of morbid pilgrimage. What were
they better than? What made them complete? How did
they survive each day, knowing that what they were
born with could so easily have been twisted into a
simple tourist trap? These questions were answered
once through that heavy curtain.*

"I've never heard of this place," the woman says,
dismissing my tale with casual sip from her mug. The
dirty man slides closer.

*Our names would be printed as donators or
personal collectors or generous contributors under
each exhibit and every tourist, every truck driver,
every dreamer would go home with the names Jackson
Jacoby and Gina Gertrude on their lips. A face didn't*

matter. A name is all anyone really needs.

Raised with a bound foot—I'm talking dynastic Chinese, crazy bound shit—Gina's personal contribution was obvious. I had nothing, aside from the leftovers of this ear—a torch accident, I say when the drivers lean in—but I knew a man named Marion Garza who had been a boxer in Chihuahua for a number of years before escaping up here to cut the necks of cattle at a big beef packing plant back west. He had a crazy ear, something anyone wouldn't mind paying five bucks to see. I know firsthand the attention a fucked up ear gets.

We would start with her foot, and then use that money to tear up the entire country, taking parts from people who had no business hoarding them. We kept a list of dream parts discovered in magazines and daytime TV talk shows: a blind man with aniridia—he wouldn't miss the eye; a child with a non-typical genital appearance the parents would be happy to forfeit; and my personal favorite, a middle-aged woman's head with Crouzon Syndrome, a rare condition resulting from premature fusion of the sutures of the skull causing bulging eyes, underdeveloped jaw, and an arched nose. Even more spectacular was that this woman had Acanthosis Nigricans—dark, rough patches of skin tucked into the folds of the body, discoloration of the flesh as an infant,—a condition that despite statistics happened to tag along with her messed-up head. And of course

Marion Garza's ear.

We had crazy plans for nabbing this beautiful cauliflower ear. We thought of burglarizing his home, waiting at his car, calling on the telephone like we were some scientific organization wanting to study his ear—then we would jump him when he came down to our fake offices. We even thought of asking the man for it but passed, assuming we'd have to cut him in on the money and now, I realize, even two ways was too much for Gina. Goddamn Gina.

When I saw the foot floating there in that jar I not only sensed the weight of money fade from my back pocket but, even more depressing perhaps, I felt rejected by the one path I thought had been so clearly paved. We weren't an item—nothing like that—but we were of a single interest, a single motivation: to make a name, and some change in the process. And we were there to do it together, Gina and Jackson, Bonnie and Clyde, Mickey and Mallory. We were a family, it felt for those first few months of planning. Oedipus and Jocasta. Then we fell apart.

She had the startup capital—her foot,—I'll give her that, and maybe because of that she felt her role was in some way superior to mine. But I was the salesman with a mouth full of honest words, a fat bank of deal-sealing smiles, and one day a clean suit to house the two. We were close. We were ready. But that fucking Marion Garza and the shit he must've said, the shit she must've believed.

The woman with living hair slurps back the last of her coffee, stands, dusts crumbs from her cleavage. Her skin ripples like water. "Where are they now?"

"Close."

She sets the empty mug on her empty plate and walks away, ending our friendship with a casual nod. Her man follows her down a hallway toward the showers.

The dirty man slides into the warmth the others left behind.

"Does a place like that really exist?" he asks. His breath smells of cat piss and mold, and his tongue weaves between sparse teeth as he talks.

"The museum?"

"Yeah." He reaches back for a forgotten biscuit from the clean man's plate and shoves it into his own breast pocket.

"There's just a few. Only some don't pay as well. You've got to know the trade."

The man stuffs a handful of napkins into his pants pocket. He shoves salt and pepper shakers in his socks, capping the holes with more napkins. He leaves exact change for his meal then stands and leans close enough to me for fugitive stink to infect my shirt. "Can I show you something?"

"I've got a tight schedule. I'm headed east."

The man scratches his arm. "I think I have a part for you."

I spoon in the final bite of gravy and wipe my mouth with my sleeve. "In that case."

"This way," he says and maneuvers out a rear door, ending near a dumpster, the area lit only by the distant parking lot lights. The evening air has stiffened since entering the diner, but I don't mind. The dirty man seems okay with it, seems at home in the cold.

"Don't scream," he says then pulls up his shirt to reveal a large mass the color of olives. He grabs me by the wrist and rubs my fingers over the skin. Its texture vibrates my hand like a cheese grater might. "How much?" he says. "If I went to one of those places how much do you think it would go for?" The mass covers the entire left side of his belly. "I'd like to do something special for my family. Maybe buy my mom a bike."

I examine the potential relic, pulling him closer to the light. I twist him, feel the skin like it matters, and pretend to figure math in my head.

"Not much." I lie. "Not enough to impress anyone, at least."

His face drops. He pulls his shirt down and holds his belly like an offended child. "People always notice it," he tries.

"What the fuck is it?"

"My twin," he says. "I've named it Monica."

I forego shock in favor of composure, despite my immediate morbid fascination. "A fetus-in-fetu. I've read about those. You'll have to do something to validate that thing, though. Photograph it in the right light; make it look like a celebrity. Get some news coverage. If you have a story ready for them that they can sell, you'll get a little more." I can see the wheels cranking. "But still not much."

He stares down. It's been with him since birth, through school, through work, through whatever family he's given up to be a driver. He's had this one crutch, this one go-to complaint for however the world taunts him, and here he is now, considering his life prior a waste. "Not much is enough." He introduces himself as Roy.

"With my connections you'll get four times what you could get on your own." We shake on it.

The back door to the restaurant swings open and out pops a large man with a greasy blue shirt draping his torso and a net corralling his erratic hair. He carries a barrel of cabbage leaves and corn husks. I help him to the dumpster. He thanks me. "This is a specimen," I say to Roy. "Look at that eye. What do you see?"

The cook and the dirty man give me equally confused glares.

"A lazy eye like that could produce gas money to either coast and back." The cook pulls away, but smiles a bit, still, for being praised. "This is what you're fighting against. Nobody wants to be blind. Some people say the Blue Bouquet has one of the creator's own eyes in it."

"What's the Blue Bouquet?"

"Shit man, get out once in a while. Do something, like my good man here," and I motion toward the cook.

The cook, proud though confused, steps away and disappears through the back door of the restaurant. He had no lazy eye, but I bet on the dirty man not knowing what a fucking lazy eye even is.

Roy nods like he's taken the advice to heart. In the darkness behind the restaurant he reminds me of Creg, his round cheeks, his black hair, his homesickness.

"I'm on my way to a shop out east," I say. "If you've got nothing else to do you can come along. I'll find you a good price for that twin."

Pulling a chuck from the biscuit in his pocket he says, "Thanks," then tosses the bite into the dark hole of his mouth.

I ask him if his truck will be alright left alone for a week or so. He nods. We climb into mine, I put the bitch into gear, and let the smooth black current carry us eastward.

⊞

After almost an hour of silence I notice the dirty man picking at a scab, blood everywhere. I punch his hand away.

"Sorry," he says.

"It's fine. Don't worry. Maybe just concentrate on finding an angle. How are you going to sell it?"

He shrugs and pops into his mouth a few of the peanuts I brought out from the back of the truck before we left the BETO parking lot.

"Have you won any contests?" I ask.

"Long jump one year in junior high," he says, excited.

"You have any special skills?"

"No."

"We could sell your family life. Were you ever beaten? Raped? Drugged?"

"I had a pretty nice childhood, actually. Even with this." He pats his belly.

"That's disappointing. A nice childhood won't work. Come up with something," I say. "Lie if you have to. Find a story and stick with it. Believe it so hard that every tourist will have to believe it as well." I push and I push, but I fear I'm pushing into empty space. "You a Saint?" I ask him.

"No. I think I'm German mostly."

Oh, if I had a gun.

"We can fake it." I hand him a pen. "You're a Saint. Start there and try to have something by the time the sun comes up."

He grabs the pen enthusiastically but settles quickly. "Paper?"

The only paper I have is Creg's notebook. With

trepidation, I hand it to the dirty man and say, "write small."

He chews the pen for a few minutes then, for no apparent reason, offers a friendly pat on my shoulder. "Stories and driving. It'll be just like those Cadbury Tales, huh, pardoner?"

"That's right, *partner*. Like those *Canterbury Tales*." He pulls the pen from his mouth, seems offended by my corrections for a moment, but he did remind me of a small box of Easter-leftover chocolate crème eggs in the back, so I forget his offense quickly. I have him take the wheel.

"Where we headed?" he yells.

"Just straight."

"Can't. I've got a T-intersection. We going on into Columbia or up to Unionville?"

"Which one is toward Delaware?" I ask.

"Columbia, I think," the dirty man says.

"Sounds good."

"I like Columbia," he says. "I've got a sister in Columbia."

I come back, take over the driver's seat, and hand the man an egg, melted but still solid enough to chew. "You seen her in a while?"

"It's been a few years. She had a lung removed. Smoking," then he stops. He slaps my shoulder and says, "Maybe she still has it. A black lung will go for a few cents, right?"

I let an egg fall apart in my mouth. "Sure."

"Sorry," Roy says.

"About?"

"I'm not a truck driver. I lied. I make cabinets. Nobody cares about custom work anymore. They go to Home Depot and—"

"Just write," I say.

We switch seats on the fly. He opens Creg's notebook to blank back page and begins writing.

The afternoon opens with steam, dedicated birds fly in a staggered V above us. For hours we ride east into the fall season, hit with this heat hidden since July. A commentator on the radio says the freak heat is concerning. I tell Roy to take the wheel, breaking the swap with a yawn. We switch seats, barely slowing the truck at all, and when seated I immediately hang my head out the passenger window, drying the sweat on my forehead with the steamy passing wind. I close my eyes to hope for a dream in which I'm floating on cold clouds.

All the way into Columbia, Roy doesn't shut up about his sister's black lung. He insists that he "knew she got cancer for a reason," and "she was always one to look out for her family." I can barely close my eyes without being shaken to attention by an anecdote about the first time his sister tried smoking, or the color they named her phlegm when he was little: Rancid Spinach. Every few tales he breaks with an offer of weed and West Coast Turnarounds. I deny both, needing sleep, not chemically modified community.

By the time we arrive in Columbia Roy had developed a lengthy list of possible purchases he would make with the lung money. He denies me more than a single moment to wake before dumping the list on me. He speeds through the items, from boats to exotic pets to guitars, all gifts for his family he says, barely a breath taken. "Cross more speed pills off that list," I tell him. He does.

His niece answers the door in Columbia, a homely, brown-haired girl that, by her confused reaction to Roy's presence had no idea he was coming and likely mistakes him for a capital-S Stranger, touting a look dramatically misplaced amid the kempt suburban house, landscaped and all. When she turns, screaming for her dad, I ask Roy if he bothered calling ahead. "Her mother's my sister," he says.

Half a cup of coffee into this reunion I find out that Roy's sister died seven months ago due to complications with her cancer treatment. The topic breaks the father down to tears. The girl cries too though motivated less likely by her mother's death than by the road weary strangers slouched on her couch.

"It's good coffee," Roy says and forces a tear of

his own.

The father thanks him, then after an awkward silence he stands and says, "if that's all then..." The father lets implication fill the fading words.

"Actually, I was wondering if I could get something Lynda had."

The father shrugs.

"A matchbook," he says which sounds more ridiculous to me than a cancerous lung but then quantifies the item by saying, "signed by Neil Diamond. It's pretty rare."

His brother-in-law ultimately gives in, though not without a warning against staying too long. "We've got a dance recital to get to," he says. "In an hour."

"No problem," Roy says, already sniffing around the master bedroom closet. After a few minutes he descends into the basement then climbs the attic ladder, coming back from each hole angry.

I offer the brother-in-law talk so small I sweat. "What do you do?" I ask.

"Computer stuff."

"You like it?"

"A job is a job."

"I agree completely," I say and loosen slightly. This man, his daughter, they exist shined by a death's patina, where things like jobs have a true irrelevance. "There're more important things than jobs," I say. The father nods. I look to the girl, say "I lost my mom, too," and before the exchange can mature, below us, above us, cardboard tears and tape rips. The destruction lifts the father from the couch.

Before the man is fully upright Roy runs from the hallway, coated in dust and sweat says, "Can't find it," a package poorly concealed under his arm. He grabs my wrist en-route to the front door and drags me away with him. I lock eyes with the girl for a moment, she with me, a shared moment between us. She clings to her father's leg, all her strength transferred to the man's thigh. I take her white knuckles and her father's reciprocated embrace with perhaps a spot of jealously. She is lifetimes ahead of me.

Within two breaths we were back in the truck, ignoring the father's demand for the return of whatever it is Roy has stolen. He tosses the package to the passenger floorboard and tells me to drive.

"I didn't think she kept it," he says after a few miles spent regaining our breath. "I was hoping, sure, but the truth is I haven't seen any of those three in a while. They don't like me coming around."

"What's in the bag?"

Roy grins. He holds the lip of the bag steady and pulls out a jar, yellow and black suspended in clear liquid."

"Bullshit," I say, impressed. "Let me see that," and I reach for the jar and pull Roy's free hand to the steering wheel. He alternates quick glances to the road and longer gazes to me as I inspect the specimen. Mineral spirits and a few oily chamois clothes. "This isn't a fucking lung," I say. "I can see the oil reflecting the light."

"No," he says and reaches for a dashboard map light. "That's the alveolar spaces having been taken over by macrophages. Those scavenger cells are filling with impurities from the smoke." He notices the astonishment his vocabulary arises in me, and justifies his speech: "When your sister has had lung cancer for half of your life, you pick up on a bit of the terminology," he says.

He leans in and grabs for the jar. I refuse to let it go. "I can see the fibers of the cloth," I say.

"That's the cancerous tissue." He points out this topography. "The stuff that looks like bread mold."

I remember my conversation with Tammy in the parking lot of Town Royale, justifying myself in the eyes of a stranger. Kindreds, Roy and I. I take a chance: "What's the gap you are trying to fill?" He pulls back. "Passing off a dirty rag as a diseased lung."

"It *is* a lung."

I sigh. "Fine, I'll go first. My mother kicked me out when I was ten. I slept on couches, benches, in ditches and did everything short of kill house pets in order to eat. My uncle took me in during the worst of it, but because I was alone for most of my life I never had the opportunity to know if what I was doing truly mattered. Validation is a basic need in all of us.

If you don't get it as a kid, you try getting it as a teenager. If you don't get it as a teenager, you try getting it as a twenty-two year old deformed, vagabond. My uncle says I have 'nomadic roots' but that implies roots of some kind. I've never had roots. I've never had a home life to point me where I needed to go. I've never had a destination, until recently."

The road flows below us for a few blinks. "I just think it looks close enough to fool someone, is all." He dilutes the tension with a breathy chuckle. "I still call my mom about every week."

Then, like the world knew we needed the diversion, a single bird hits the GreenAmerica truck windshield, cracks it deep, and yellow goop slides up the glass. "Yeah, we can probably sell it," I say. The bird's eye and beak drags upward through its pureed organs, never again to be part of a V formation.

FOURTEEN

The Adventures of Sir Potato and
Bucket Boy

I'm straddling the state line into Illinois. Some call it the official end of the West, some the heart of the Midwest. I have no preference for terminology outside the East. Delaware. I dial Kevin's mother for a progress update during a refuel. Her voice nourishes this weary traveler. Before hanging up I tell Kevin's mother I love her, and her vibrato tears filter though like the static of a loose wire somewhere out there between us, windblown against a telephone pole or the ground, tempting total disconnection.

Roy calls his brother-in-law to apologize but can't get two words out before the line goes dead. I shrug like I care, but don't have the words to craft the faux sentiment. Roy is clearly disheveled, verging on tears I swear, and could use comfort of any kind, but I just don't have any to spare.

Our dietary regimen consisted of cheese crackers, Snyder's Hotdog flavored potato chips, and Pop-Tarts for the initial leg of the trip. When the food choices got slim we made more frequent stops at highway diners and chain restaurants. Our favorite was a fast-food joint called The Potato Bucket, not for the mediocre food, but for the paper place mats decorated in funny comics depicting the adventures of Sir Potato and Bucket Boy. They became our alter egos for a few states until suddenly, simultaneously, we recognized how ridiculous the charade was. For two hours after this realization we fought over who started it.

We were two travelers. Our destination was my destination. At least this was the way I ride it until after a heavy silence somewhere near Alton, Roy turns to me and asks what city the next part museum is in. "I really just want to get my money and be on my way to tell you the truth," he says, his reluctance and discomfort keeping the words soft.

"Majorville," I blurt, assuming a town with a name like that has to one, exist and two, be known for something.

"What state is that in?"

"It's just a little more east. Pennsylvania, if I remember right."

"Are you sure? I haven't seen any signs or anything."

"Majorville," I repeat.

"How will they remove her?" he asks.

"Her?" I say.

He's lifted his shirt, dances his fingers around his

scars. "I don't know. I just figured. I call her Monica."

The day is hot, hot like this beginning of December is a lie. I've got the window down and the heat only fills my lungs with steam. Roy has removed his shirt, revealing among his tattoos, scars, and fetus-in-fetu sibling, a stink worse than any burning blood. I'd ask him about Monica, but conversation would mean actually trying, and honestly I couldn't handle it.

Roy reaches to the radio for the volume knob. A song I remember hearing when I was younger fades to silence. Over the wind his words are just mutters. "What?"

"I said, maybe I'll have you down to the condo sometime. When I buy one with the lung money—" but stops when we he sees that we are riding over a lake. Its surface chops, agitated by more boats than an Illinois December day should ever know. Nobody swims. The water, unlike the air, remains true to the standard December temperature. Then a catamaran capsizes after interrupting the path of a large fishing boat. Quick, like it didn't even happen. A horn from an oncoming minivan brings Roy back to the road.

"Fuck, Roy."

He apologizes. "I've always wanted a speedboat." He takes a bite of a Zero bar. "You think I'll get enough for a speedboat, too?"

After slowing my panic to slow breaths I tell him, "That depends on what kind of story you've got. All that matters is the story." I'm already building a story of my own about the wrecked catamaran.

"I think you'll like it," he says. "So, I'm a Saint, like you said. Good heart, honor, respect, all that. But my secret is that I've never had a mother. She left when I was younger, off to get work acting in Spanish TV shows." He pauses, grins. "I went down to Mexico looking for her, but came into trouble with an anti-America militia. They burned me, torched me, and tried to take Monica but suddenly the image of the Virgin Mary appeared." He waits for my reaction, the grin still glowing. "I'm willing to get the image of the Virgin Mary on there somehow, if it would help. Maybe I could brand it on there, like with what ranchers use for livestock." The bird guts from earlier have hardened to the windshield by this point, now crystallized and translucent like a fractured stained-glass window. "I took the missing mother and Spanish TV thing from your notebook."

"I couldn't tell," I say flatly.

"Yeah," he throws it to me. "You really know how to take the problem of your missing mother and twist it into something psychotic. It's brilliant."

I lift the notebook. Roy's green ink bleeds over Creg's hunt. The care my friend had taken to represent his mother throughout these pages is buried now, abused by Roy's dirty fucking hand. The notebook represented the only promising path Creg had ever known. He has no voice on the phone. He has no road leading to Delaware. He has a notebook, a television set, and hope riding on jump cuts and camera changes.

"You can't have that story," I say to him.

"The Potato Bucket is passing through me," he says, oblivious to my comment. "If you care for your upholstery you won't mind a pit stop." He pulls into a gas station at the edge of a junction town called Blank. While Roy is occupied in the restroom I engage the attendant, thinking really only of Creg and how much I suddenly understand of the man. "How'd the name Blank come about?"

"Some Colonel, I think," the attendant responds.

He offers nothing else so to escape my growing unease I reach down and grab two packs of gum. "This is it," I throw down a five dollar bill. He hands me my change, wishes me a "fine day." I ask about a payphone before stuffing the gum in my pocket, throwing back my own "you too."

Kevin's mother materializes on the line, and I'm spilling all the news of my destination, a confirmed journey to Delaware. She erupts with joy. It feels like a hug through all the static. "We'll have a big meal," she says. "I'll get everyone up here for the reunion. Uncle Bill, Samantha, Keenan, everyone."

"That's okay," I say.

I can hear Kevin's mother chewing something. Something crunchy. "When?" she asks.

"There's this guy I have to get rid of sometime

between here and there. He has this birth defect, a dead twin sticking out of his belly and honestly, it fucks with my head."

"Kevin," she hisses. "Such language."

"This guy has a cheese grater looking scar covering his entire gut. I'll be rid of him soon, though. He thinks we're headed for another part museum, but I don't know."

"Call again soon," she pleads.

"I love you," and before I hear the sentiment's return I feel a warm grip on the back of my neck.

"You fucker," Roy yells. "You dragged me all the way out here." His hands squeeze around my throat. They smell nothing like soap. "I could've been looking on my own this whole time. I might've had my condo and my boat by now."

I try to explain as he continues to squeeze. He is yelling, fading, as the words quiet to a hush and the world between us blurs to black.

I wake up underneath the payphone with nothing but my clothes and a headache. It's alright, really. With all that bullshit I fed him he won't get but three states before giving up. If there is one thing I can do well it's bullshitting.

FIFTEEN

Bleeding Raspberry Filling and Swallowing Percocets

I am not alone for long. I spot the familiar shape of the GreenAmerica truck. Its silhouette, backed by the rising sun, revitalizes me after a night of walking.

I assume the vision a mirage at first and berate myself as punishment for the senseless hope. But a mirage would come with fuel. And keys. The truck's tank is empty, the keys are gone, but I capitalize on the simple presence of something real, and I touch the sun-hot metal. Despite the burn and the pain I still believe in vindication: Roy got far, but he didn't get where he wanted to go.

I check the back of the truck to ensure my rouge passenger isn't waiting for me. He's gone, and aside from a few empty snack cake racks and one flat tire there's no tell of his existence at all. I walk back to the driver's cab. Creg's notebook sits on the dashboard. A quick flip through its pages reveals the final trace of Roy. His scribbled stories trail off on the final pages.

Cars pass, the drivers coughing, sneezing, yelling at passengers, doing whatever to skip eye contact with this deserted traveler. Feeling the first pangs of real hunger—simple nagging hunger having come and gone many miles back—I enter the back of the truck for a few crème pies. I fill my pockets, ready myself for a slow road ahead. In the corner of the truck, beyond a barricade of tumbled muffin bites, I notice a small hoard of trial mix. I move to fill my pockets fuller when, like an eager pilgrim, I flatten a poor Zinger, its raspberry filling bleeding through the floor of the truck to the earth below. I get an idea.

Fifteen minutes later I'm running out of and around the truck like a spastic blood-high mosquito.

"Help!" I yell, "I need a doctor. I need an ambulance." I'm baiting a hero with my arm decorated in raspberry filling. But cars still pass. The people inside take interest, at least, but still they drive, giving their engines gas and leaving me with their dry exhaust.

As more vehicles pop over the horizon I extend the fruit filling spread to my shirt, my face, everywhere, and scream like the injury is two minutes to gangrenous; I'm two minutes to vulture food. At first I yell actual words but coming close to the end of my vocabulary of synonyms for *ouch*, I resort to wailing, whining, and expletives. When these fail I lie at the shoulder and fake near-death. I hook a traveler in no time. A hero, I suppose, is easiest when the damsel can't scream.

...to keep that woman from having a child...

The scene hits me like a walking dream. Something from my past. Something intangible yet forever present. My arms, bloody, aren't my arms. They are another son's arms. The raspberry goop hardens by the heat, pulling the hairs from my skin in quick, painful bursts. The abandoned truck, the red pouring from my body, these images don't belong only to me. They are of another life entirely...

But I'm on the ground, back to the hero above me, though I can't shake the life I just embodied. I felt even beyond Kevin.

First this dumb bastard attempts CPR. His ignorance is a true godsend as he doesn't push deep enough to even crack my chest, let alone start my heart. When this fails he goes in for mouth-to-mouth, and I take it—I need the ride. At this point full consciousness would mean his success, not mine, and there's no telling how fast this man might leave me, ready to tell this tale of heroism to drunk women in dark bars. His mustache tickles. His breath tastes like cat urine and smoke. Through the tiny slits I've left for my eyes I see his giant, strung-out, drug-stretched pupils.

"You're not going on me," he screams. "Not today. No. You've got too much to live for," and on and on he goes. He lifts me with PCP strength and takes the time to buckle me in, to dust off my shirt and wipe a bit of raspberry blood from my arm. "We'll take care of you," he says to my limp body.

To waken now might destroy the potential miles I could get from this man, and who knows how dangerous he may be, so I stay unconscious. I flop to the divots in the road and bounce between the window and this man's shoulder as his sharp turns dictate.

"This doesn't happen too often," he says to me—to himself, to the empty road. "Find a body on the road and stop to pick it up. But who knows? Maybe you got some money. Maybe your family's got some money and we'll see a bit of a reward for you. Can't say that's my intention. Nope. I can't. I just want to show a bit of compassion, but lord knows,"—he sniffles and checks his rearview, his movements quick like a fly's beating wings—"a few bucks would help me out. And if you're poor I could do the talk show circuit. They pay in prizes. Groceries, vacations, big TVs, and even a whole new house I saw once. Fucking family didn't do nothing. Just had retarded kids is all. But I'm not complaining. I couldn't raise a retard. Nobody could, really. Seems the retard would be the one doin' the raisin' and I'm grown up enough for two lifetimes."

He flips through a few radio stations until an elevator jazz number drips from the cracking speakers.

"I saw a show once where a father killed himself,

150

then the mother tried"—a long car horn and a quick jerk of the wheel puts the driver back into his lane. He huffs a few deep breathes, swallows something from his pocket, and continues with his story—"but she didn't see it through, and the whole country felt for this woman, what a brave woman she was for deciding to live and to support her kids. A single mother, they kept sayin' and crying and whining about how tough it's got to be. But she tried to quit. She had the knife halfway into her gut, but the handle broke off—some piece of shit plastic-handled turd—and she couldn't get the rest in there. Her kid came and saw it, bothered 911 about it, and for all this she got a brand new car, a new house, and a vacation. Tell you what, that sets a new standard for what people like me got to do. We used to have to *do* something. Now we just got to cry about what's been *done* to us."

He keeps talking, lighting a joint the size of a pencil, humming to the poor jazz, drumming his way through the dying daylight. But we're still headed east. I can pretend to be unconscious all the way to Delaware if I have to.

"Maybe if I knew for sure you was somebody important, like I heard about you doin' something big, then I wouldn't care about the talk show circuit. I could just go on telling people I meet about the time I found *that guy* on the side of the road...with his pants down, I'll say, and covered in semen the way they tag their killed down in the cities. I saw a special on Channel 9 about it one year, about how when some gang nigger gets killed the ones doing the killing circle around him and just let loose, ejaculate all over him. They don't care about all their boys watchin'. They just paint that nigger white."

The joint extinguishes itself. He relights and swallows back a cough.

"I'll take my rounds on the news, talking about how you was dyin' when I found you but by the time we get to any hospital you ain't breathin'. You'll be like a celebrity. You'll be huge. And I'll be huge right there along with you. I don't want to make you up like I have to, but I've got a family to support."

But the smoke is too much and I cough loud, shooting raspberry phlegm across the windshield and dashboard.

"Holy fuck," the man yells. He turns stern, eager to save, gases the engine until were passing cars quick enough to make returning to the right lane a waste. "We'll get you somewhere, don't worry."

"My arm," I say to keep the charade going. It sounds to me like *"my mom."*

"We'll do it. We'll do it ..." He repeats this loud, then falls to soft sputters of breath like he is drifting to sleep. I kick him and blame the pain.

He claims a long stretch of deserted road, perfect for emergency driving. Although our speed remains at nauseating near-triple digits the environment inside this pickup truck cab feels unusually composed, like we've established equilibrium. He hands me the joint, saying, "This'll keep you wet till we find a hospital. We're just inside Olden. I know a place around here." While I contemplate his odd usage of *wet* he continues. "This might sound sorta fucked up about now, but you wouldn't happen to be a celebri—"

A honk. A swerve. A motorcycle against the driver-side door and for real my arm is fucked. The purple raspberry filling deepens with the dye of true blood.

Am I airborne, spinning?

We've slid into a ditch. The man sprawls unconscious against the steering wheel. The motorcyclist has disappeared. I manage my way out of the truck but not without swiping the driver's wallet and unrolling him from his massive coat. I wear the coat to keep my mangled arm hidden until I can find a place to blame for this injury.

An old friend, he managed a large department store, told me that eighty-seven percent of people injured at his store had no medical insurance.

My arm swells as my sight fades out, fades in...

When I walk through the front door of a nearby store, a slow, elderly man in a blue smock and a blurry nametag smiles and yawns. I am in pain, almost debilitating now that the cold, outdoor air isn't numbing my arm. But being so close to so many ways to feign injury I grit my teeth and smile.

My first instinct is to hit the power tools section. I could surely displace my injury there. But by the aisle signs hanging from the ceiling, the tools are in the back corner and judging by the way the world around me fades and blurs, I need something now. The swelling coat around my arm is getting heavy.

But then I see a nearby clearance deal: fireproof safes at 30 dollars.

I pay a passing green-haired kid five dollars to stack a few of the safes on top of me. He offers to tip the entire display over my arm for ten. I accept. But to not scream, to not stab the kid as he goes about arranging the load with absolutely no concern for my injured arm is difficult. Though in his defense, he works quickly before any shoppers pass. He finishes and runs off with his money. I finally let the pain be known.

I'm yelling. I am screaming blood. Children cry around me. People try to help, but I kick them away until a manager is able to see these results of a failed gondola. After full minutes a woman in a blue vest appears, speaking into a static radio, and asks me if I'm alright.

"My arm," I yell. "I think it's broken."

She moves the box away.

"You need to stack these things better," I say. "Someone could have been killed."

A man with a mop is called, "bodily fluids," the

woman says over her radio. Within minutes a fat fuck with a red garbage bag shows up. Minutes more and I'm being strapped to a gurney and fed oxygen. I have no adrenaline left. My lips fold under my teeth and my fingers pull to loose fists. The air tastes like sweat and …

⊞

"… and I couldn't go to a hospital because Marion Garza and Gina could track me by the insurance claim. They've got friends." What the hell did I just say?

"My name is Natalie," I hear. "I'm not Kevin's mother."

The air smells like chemicals and sweat. I hear the names of doctors through overhead loudspeakers. "I'm sorry," I hear myself say. "I didn't mean to be Kevin. I just thought you might want me to be."

"Natalie," the voice says, calm, reassuring.

I've been spilling words like they don't matter.

"You were frantic," the ugly blur says. She says they had to fill me with gas to calm me enough to set the bone, that I had suffered only a simple greenstick fracture, that I'll be fine in a couple weeks. "You'll still be able to steal ears," she says with a grin.

How much have I said?

"How many hit-and-runs *have* you been involved in," the blur asks?

"More than this one, it feels like," I offer, grinning away the truth behind the statement.

"Well, you made it to a hospital, anyway," one of them says, elevating the bed. She turns to the door, laughing with the other blur. Together they leave me alone.

With the driver's cash—a nice stack—I fill a prescription for Percocet the next morning and head into the heart of this town called Olden to search for a way east.

SIXTEEN

The Bodybuilder and the Dead Man

A broken arm in a cast can't stop me from stalking and stealing a swerving van from a driver too drunk to know he's been had. I leave him in the ditch. He's passed out before he hits the grass. The van smells of paper and ink, is filled with bound stacks of crisp newspapers.

I return to scope the crash site—the perps always do, I heard somewhere—and meet a man in a yellow suit with scrub brushes and a power hose. I ask him about the wreck. "I only clean these failures up," he says and goes back to cleaning what was once me, once the driver, once the motorcyclist; now a single mess. I watch him for a few minutes, he doesn't seem to mind. When he finally drives away, he's left only black rubber tattooed into the pavement too deep to pry out. Not bad for stains set overnight.

The van has the name of the newspaper, *The Olden Republic*, painted in grandiose letters on the side. This town is too small not to notice one of its own escaping, so when I come to a local resident walking a dog, or jogging, or sitting on a porch, I wave and smile in ways strangers never could. Smiles are like the underground railroad through small towns.

To fill my gut before getting too far on the road I stop at a straggling diner on the edge of a neighboring town. My world is full of retired farmers and next-gen understudies. I take a seat in eyesight of the van. Not two sips into my coffee a giant man bursts though the door—a stranger, judging by the instant silence—and he sits only two stools to my left. I don't like the way he smells.

He orders water and a bowl of fruit. Two hard-boiled eggs. Bran cereal. Four slices of toast, no butter. A glass of skim milk.

I order the special, not knowing what the special is, and focus on not wetting myself. This man dominates the room like a felled tree just split the diner in two. The sole waitress drops my order in front me. I am cheek deep into the bowl of runny clam chowder when between slurps I hear the man say, "No fucking way," like he's just discovered masturbation. By the time he repeats *way* I look up to see this tan-faced Hulk reaching out to touch what's left of my ear. "I figured I could look all the way to your brains," he says.

"Excuse me?" I curb any possible harshness in my voice with a meek smile. He smells like a dead cow, like a three-month road trip without direction; just random sites and bathroom breaks in ditches.

"What happened to it?"

"Why?"

"You can't have an ear like that and not expect a few questions."

I just stare at him for a few beats, searching for hints of a joke. I find none. "Torch accident."

"Serious?" He leans closer.

I just smile and show off the other ear as a point of comparison. Awe stretches his grin wider.

Listen. This girl I know, Gina, she's a lot lizard most of the time because truckers always seem to have the most interesting deformities. I don't know this for a fact, but I've got to say it would be one hell of a coincidence. I've never met a driver without some shit wrong with him; scars, bedsores, hemorrhoids, and even athlete's foot, ironically.

When I first met Gina she asked me about my ear. I was itching for some ass so I told her what she wanted to hear. I told her some bullshit hero story about saving orphan or animals; I don't remember. This really got her going. And when she was close, breathing against my neck and I could feel the heat all over, I told her I had kept the ear. A memento. Turns out I was just what she was looking for. She wasn't just kinky, she was weird outside the sack, too. She also had this thing where she went all over the place stealing body parts and selling them to freak roadside museums.

He pops a large grape into his mouth. "Those things don't exist."

She thought I might be interested in making some money. And she was right. I offered her a cut of the money, but until then I would do whatever she needed me to do. Like I said, I was itching. But when she found out I really didn't have my dead ear anymore she split. Soon as she got the chance she jumped in with this trucker named Marion Garza; his ear was all fucked up from his days as a boxer in Mexico. One night she cut the damn dead ear off, lobe and all, and had the nerve to sell it without me. "You?"

He blows his nose into a napkin, tucks the red ball under his plate. "I'm looking for work. Maybe I'll go a little more north and dodge the draft. I've got options."

"We don't have a draft."

"We'll always have a draft. Just because the government isn't drawing birthdates doesn't mean we aren't being picked at some other way," and he lets an awkward silence pass, a silence I wouldn't dare interrupt. "I also tour the bodybuilding circuit," he says. "But I'm getting old." He fills me in on his life so far, his first marriage, his second marriage, the bodybuilding competitions, his frequent wins, his third marriage. "The regime is stressing this old fucker out. I've quit the testosterone injections. Now I'm just cutting my losses where I can. Want some pills? I've got Dianabol, Wistrol, and even some Percocet. By the looks of your arm you could use some."

I pull out my own bottle of pills, pop a couple in my mouth while I'm thinking about it, and say, "Maybe later." By the rate I'm destroying this first bottle I mean the offer.

"I'm Jackson Jacoby," by the way." I offer my good hand for a shake.

"Robert," he says, accepting my hand.

"Robert what?"

"Can't tell you that," he says. "It's a trademark thing. You don't own me."

I laugh. He doesn't.

"But we can be like brothers." He throws his arm toward me, knocking chowder down the front of my shirt. He passes me a napkin.

Halfway through my bowl Robert pays for my meal and pulls me from my stool. "Let's hit the town for a while," he says. He grabs my bill before I can and pulls himself free from my booth.

"I can't," I say, bracing for retaliation. "I'm stealing the *Olden Republic's* van."

"Nice." He smiles. "Let's fucking get going then."

Let's? He's a man like me, finding family where it finds him, but what sort of family do we have to offer each other? Having a new passenger might be nice, though.

So, I agree and before I can say anything else,

we're standing in the parking lot just as a late model Ford Escort backs into the van's rear taillight. Like it's instinctual, Robert darts after the Escort. I watch in awe as he nearly grabs onto the bumper before he finally slows.

I yell, "He's probably drunk. It's not my van anyway."

"Fuck no," he says, sweating cannonballs. "We're going after him." He nods me to his own vehicle, a small, sporty car with a moon roof. We get in and tail the escapee by a few hundred feet until arriving at a small home with bright, plastic toys in the front yard. We coast by just as the man's child greets him at the front door. Robert pops a pill, chews it like candy. "Tonight," he says. "We'll come back tonight."

The rest of the afternoon I spend trying to convince Robert that a broken taillight is an easy fix, reminding him often that I stole the van to begin with. We move the van to a secluded access road not far from the diner. Robert insists we spend the wait bowling; his pupils have dilated, so I figure my safest option is to relent and appease the man's bowling fetish for a few hours. Every few minutes or so I step easy into another attempt at dissuading him from returning to Ford Escort man's house. When he grabs me by the throat—after a three-strike turkey I managed on accident—and tells me he won't let jerks like that stomp all over me, I finally give up. The following game I set the alley record for gutters.

So I ask him what he plans on doing. If I can't stop him maybe I can guide him elsewhere.

"It'll be an adventure," he says, his face glossy with sweat, his neck boiling with acne. When he knocks over a pin the entire alley takes notice. His celebratory rituals are that vocal.

"How much of an adventure?" I ask.

"We'll swing by and see what comes to mind. Start thinking."

I pretend. Between faux suggestions—egg the home, gas the lawn, prank phone calls— I'm devising an emergency escape plan which includes the possibility of physically incapacitating this large man—includes but offers no probable method of execution.

I'm thinking of running. I'm thinking of excusing myself to the bathroom and never coming back, but this man had pissed twelve times since our initial meeting. He'd be joining me, I'm sure. I'm thinking of telling him straight, throwing down my fear and explaining that a journey east is something I must do alone. I decide to go for it and have only, "Look, a journey east" out when he stops me.

"I'm ready, too," he says. "I have so much going for me out there. To tell you the truth I don't have many people. After my wives left me I turned to my family—a group of strangers I haven't dealt with since the first divorce. They didn't offer much." Then like he knows what I'm thinking he turns back to me from the lane after throwing his ball and says, "Thanks for going with me."

I'm not a sucker for sap. He didn't win me over with his eyes or his slight frown or his somber familial tales. In fact he didn't win me over at all. I fall into our continued friendship because all that he said I could have said. Sure, I wish this man were a bit smaller, a bit less intimidating, a bit more mellow, but he is essentially a kindred, a mirror, and via him I understand myself a bit more. I'd had a childhood like his early adulthood. I've had an adolescence like his directionless midlife. I will probably have a death like his, uneventful and alone. But until then what's wrong with enduring our invalidated lives as symbiotes?

"So where to now?" I ask as his ball flops into the gutter, limps along to the darkness behind a full, upright set of pins.

He checks his watch. "That dick's probably just lying down. We can start now and get there just as he's passing out."

When we arrive, after a ride silent aside for his humming and drumming and my nervous breathing, the house is dark. Robert turns to me. "So those ideas of yours?"

I shake my head. I'm still not against letting the hit-and-run quietly fade away but Robert, his stern eyes, his eager grin, says loud enough that forgiveness isn't an option. "We could just gas his lawn," I offer again.

He rocks in his seat for a few moments, adjusting the heat, shutting off the radio. He simmers. Then, like he's only been building courage, he opens his door quick and steps to the icy grass. "Let's just go inside. See if we can find anything in there."

I chew my lip. "Maybe I can just keep watch."

He allows the idea. Before turning to the house he leans in through the open driver's side window and says, "The abort word is *pectoral*." Then he is gone. I've never seen a tip-toeing elephant, but I feel now to have a valid frame of reference. He approaches the front door, doesn't open, then disappears around the back of the house. He isn't a friend. I would never call him that. He is companionship, though.

I swear, just as he disappears behind the house he comes running around from the other side with a package tucked like a football under his arm. I reach over and start the car.

"Let's get," he says, throwing a box on my lap, knocking my damaged arm into my ribs.

"What the hell?" I say.

"Don't even guess. It's better than you can possibly imagine."

I open what he's taken from the man's home. A bunch of videocassette. Some apparently rented from a local store and some unlabeled, possibly homemade.

"Make him pay a late fee," I say. I once again offer to egg his home.

"That's not all I took," he says and pulls out a large video camera, an old model that uses full size VHS tapes.

"I didn't know anyone still had these," I say. I try to figure him out but nothing comes. "So we make him pay a late fee *and* we erase a home movie?"

"Wait," Robert says. I don't trust his grin.

We ride slowly through the town for about an hour. Few people walking the streets drops to fewer falls to one or two, tops. Drunks. Homeless. Runaways. At each sighting Robert mumbles to himself: "No." "Too pretty." "Too young."

Then, without warning, he stops the car, jumps out, and tackles a lonely stranger. A male with a limp and a full beard. Could be homeless, drunk, some deadbeat father, or even all three. When Robert runs back with him over his shoulder and tosses him in the back seat I realize these flexible descriptions are just the reason he picked this stranger.

"Nobody will miss that fucker," Robert says, as we're off toward the edge of town.

I say nothing. I ask nothing. We've kidnapped a bum and he's unconscious in the back seat and Robert still hums, still drums his fingers against the steering wheel. I know to keep my mouth shut. He chews more pills.

We arrive at a barn a few miles outside of Olden.

No house. No farm light. No main roads. Just an empty barn. Part of me wishes the bum would wake up now, put a kink in whatever plan Robert has for the three of us.

"Help me with him," Robert says, already dragging the bum by his feet along the ground. His head bounces along the trail of rocks and dirt. "Watch it," I say lifting the man by his shoulders, my swollen arm throbbing against its cast, but I stay strong. "Please."

Once inside the barn Robert turns on a single light, just a bulb hanging in the corner. Next to it sits a mattress, a blanket, and a pillow. "This yours?" I ask.

"Sort of," he says. "For a few days it has been." Together we toss the bum onto the mattress. "On my way east I stopped here. I liked it. And I might've stayed for another couple days. The owner has me doing some winterizing to his equipment so lets me stay here for free."

"I thought you were winning bodybuilding competitions," I say. "You've got to have money left over from that."

"Not much when you have three alimony payments. Fucking laywers."

Robert steps back. He looks at the limp man, hand on chin, deep in thought as he seems to picture different poses in his head. He quickly, almost artfully, adjusts the flaccid body until it leans against the wall on its own. "No." He then tries rolling the man into a fetal position. He tries loosely wrapping him like he's suffering only a nap. When nothing satisfies him, Robert finally turns to me and says, "We need to wake him up." He kneels down and binds the man at the wrists with duct-tape from a roll I hadn't seen until then. I fear what else he might have stashed away.

"What are we doing?" I finally ask. This far in I feel I deserve at least that.

"Revenge." I watch him leave the barn and return seconds later with a bucket full of water which he dumps on the homeless man. The man mumbles awake, gurgles, chokes on the cold water.

Robert grabs me by the arm and pulls me aside. He holds up the video camera and says, "When I turn this on no talking. I'm serious. And stay out of the fucking frame."

"Who are you?" the bum asks. "What's going on?" We are so similar in our ignorance.

Robert bends down near the mattress, the camera on and secure against his eye, and then picks up a large metal pipe near his feet. He proceeds to swing it into the man's ribs, against his forearms, across his legs. He lets him spit a few sympathetic phrases between hits. The entire mess lasts only the length of my few, nauseous quivers. Robert holds and hovers the camera just over the man's feet and sweeps it up over his puddled body. He shuts off the camera then finishes the bum with a swing to the face.

Once in the car Robert removes the filmed beating from the camera, hands it to me and says to swap it out with the rented video tape. "Burn the rented tape when you get the chance," he says.

We get to the empty parking lot of the video rental store listed on the plastic case, and the world around us is empty for miles. Robert pulls close to the store, stops when the drop box is inches from me and tells me to let it go. "A time bomb," he says. "The next time someone rents this, our hit-and-runner is jailed for life. On death row if we're lucky." He smiles. I force one of my own. He returns my gesture with a full laugh that turns my stomach and keeps me silent.

Fog coats the car's windows. Slowly the streetlights and fluorescent sign of the video store blurs to an even, gentle light. We exist within a glowing box, layering breath upon the windshield. I'm not violent. I've never been violent. I've read that violence is often a symptom of a broken home, and though any home I've had could easily be considering broken, I've come to deal with those cracks and fractures in other ways. This violence scares me into silence. I open my mouth, but any vengeance I could muster, any desire to discuss the recent events civilly, is dominated by a more primitive need to simply breathe.

"Sorry," he finally says. "The steroids shift me all

over the place. Usually, I'm pretty cool, but every once-in-a-while ..."

I just silently stare straight ahead.

We leave the parking lot, leave the neighborhood. He turns to me: "But he shouldn't have hit your van like that."

I can taste acid in my throat. "I told you that it wasn't my fucking van."

We get back to the diner having endured silence for the remainder of the drive. I can see a few souls though the window, enjoying coffee and pie at the bar. Robert sneaks around back to the gravel access road and stops at the *Olden Republic* van. "Don't go," he says wiping a spot of blood from his face that he notices in his rearview mirror. "Let's drive together. We're both headed east. I'll pick you up here in the morning."

"Right," I say. I tell him I will be waiting. Instead, though, I escape town the moment his taillights disappear around a distant corner.

SEVENTEEN

Another Conversation with Mother

At the border of West Virginia I'm flagged down by a State Police Trooper claiming to be searching every vehicle entering the state for a ride-along convict named Maxwell Irving. I state that I have no passengers, but she insists on sweeping the vehicle anyway. She asks me where I'm headed.

"Delaware," I say.

"Business or personal."

"Personal. I've got a will reading to get to."

She looks at the *Olden Republic* logo on the side of the truck.

"Who's so important you got to drive all the way out there from Olden?"

Her questions would force me to the defensive, but considering Robert and last night I heed every word. "A grandfather. He was rich man."

"Sorry to hear about the loss," she says. "Good luck in Delaware." She waves me through.

A convict. A killer on the loose. I think

immediately of Robert and all the history he might have carried with him. The thought of a killer nearby, especially a killer so in need of a passenger, only forces me to push forth with the heavier burden of time. The real Kevin Masons could be home by now. He could be resting on our mother's couch, watching free cable, and eating potato chips, and I'm states away and slowly being forgotten yet again.

Motive, though. Why would Kevin Masons run away in the first place? His mother has already accepted blame with the hope that I—he—would return so what would cause such apology without a desire to be reciprocated? What did she do? He had a family, a father, a mother, and maybe siblings and a big house and a big yard and a job he enjoyed and even pets; dogs, cats, guinea pigs, maybe, so why would he abandon his family? And why wouldn't they have abandoned him first? Something broke them apart, something big, and I need to know what it is before I arrive as Kevin Masons with arms outstretched, asking for a reserved seat at the will reading for the dearly departed.

I know that a family can melt to strangers, but I have only personal experience to back that claim. I was separated by a small town, a few streets, but Kevin Masons and his mother have suffered states between them. How many different ways are there to do that?

States.

Not maps, pictures with lines and clear destinations. Full masses of land upon which real lives are lived, real families are raised, real families die.

Towns.

It hits me. I let all these questions break down to reveal a single, so much more important question. Why did Kevin's mother think he was in Veranda?

When I stop for gas I give her a call. As the phone rings, I know he could be home now, so I greet Kevin's mother with a hoarse voice, ready to claim a wrong number should I need to abort the call. But as soon as she picks up and I greet her, she shouts, "Kevin," and I can safely say, "Yeah," like I haven't been looking forward to her voice.

"You haven't called in so long. I was beginning to worry you weren't headed this way anymore."

"I'm still coming."

"Are you still in Kentucky?" she asks. "Have you left the motel yet?"

"I was never in Kentucky," I say. "I'm passing though West Virginia now."

"Right," she says. And buffered by a few moments of silence: "I just assumed Kentucky, I guess. I knew you were headed from the west and thought Kentucky was a pretty good guess."

"I was thinking, mom—"

"You're still coming, right?"

"Yeah, I'm still coming. I was just wondering

about something?"

She is silent.

"How did you know I was in Kansas?"

"Kansas," she says. "My, that's quite a distance."

"You put the ad in the paper."

"I put ads in a lot of papers."

"Why Veranda?"

"After talking to you in Mead we had no idea where you were headed. You just stopped calling so we had to start somewhere. Call it a mother's intuition."

Mead. "I guess you were right."

She hangs onto our conversation until I break it free with an unreturned *I love you.* No doubt Bodybuilder Robert is still on my trail. I want to keep my lead.

EIGHTEEN

I Know Another Kevin Masons

My first stop upon entering Mead is a phonebook hanging from a vandalized payphone outside a small grocery store. I find no listing for a Kevin Masons. He's been here before, though. Somebody has to know him.

I start at a small bar. I ask around about the name, even play the role of a private investigator, but these afternoon drunks see right through me. Not even the filthy bartender, who has probably known most everybody in this town at some point during their falls, has ever heard of him. I ask for her phone number, "In case I have further questions," I say. She tells me to fuck off.

My next stop is a general store, then a country crafts and shampoo store, where everything ends in whole dollar amounts and no shelves stand higher than five feet. I ask the young girl at the counter about Kevin. She seems to honestly ponder the name—which I appreciate more than she could possibly know—but comes up blank. I pass on asking for her number.

Then I hit another bar, a different grocery store, the senior citizens' center, a bank, a few parking lots, some motels, and even a pawn shop with the story that I've been robbed by a man named Kevin Masons and need to know if he has brought anything in. I'm given only laughter. Having my stories greeted with disbelief doesn't bother me so much. It's having them tossed aside, forgotten, like this pawn-shop bitch does that bothers me. On the way out I rip a shitty guitar from the wall and smash it to splinters against a vending machine. She yells for me to stop, but I just run. I dart past the van, down an alley, and when I stop to take a breath a police car parked around the corner opens and out oozes a giant officer. He throws me to the ground, crushes my split arm with my own weight. *Fuck.*

From inside the small holding cell, I ask his name, then leverage our burgeoning relationship to ask him if he's got any sympathy for a boy with a medical problem. "I get what are called daydreaming seizures, Officer Braggert. Most victims only freeze during episodes, but I lash out and go crazy. I thought I had time to get out," I say. "I can usually control them better."

"That was a pricey vending machine," he says. "She quoted over six-thousand dollars."

"Of course she'll over-quote it," I say. "She runs a pawn shop."

"Then hope next time you're nowhere near one when one of your *episodes* comes on."

Stuck in a tiny cell in Mead isn't where I need to be. Kevin Masons is hiding somewhere. The week isn't going well. "Six-thousand," I say. "Just call the owner, will you? See if she can deal with a straight payment."

Braggert pulls my wallet from my property envelope. He thumbs through its contents, pulling out a few bills. "This might cover the cost of my services." he says. Before calling the pawnshop owner he flips to one of the pockets in the wallet and pulls out a photograph. "Your mother?" he says holding the photo toward me.

My mother. I'd forgotten that picture was in there. She was young when it was taken. Happy. Unaware that I was inside of her. For the longest time I truly trusted that the picture would act as a source of comfort when the need for it came. I kept it close, even before I had a driver's license or cash to justify the wallet. "Yeah," I say.

"Nice," he says and shoves the picture into his pocket along with my cash.

As he walks down the hallway to the phone I am left pressed against the cold steel bars of this cell. It's an old cell. I can tell by the bars and the stink. Modern cells don't use bars. They use shatterproof glass reinforced with cage wire. I watch enough TV to know.

He comes back a few minutes later and throws my wallet back into the envelope. "She's willing to take the deal," he says. "Get your pants on and go."

My pants aren't off, but I let him have his joke. He has me sign a few papers, initial some yellow sheet, and collect my property envelope. Just as I am about the brave the world again in search of Kevin Masons I have a sudden realization of where I am and of all the people who must be catalogued here. "You need a statement, right?" I say. "You need my side of the incident, right?"

"Nope."

"But I have to," I say. I use the opportunity to explain my actions, that I was checking the pawn shop for some stolen stuff. "A guy named Kevin Masons took everything I own," I say. "I'm sure he lives in Mead. Could you at least tell me that?"

"Nope."

"What if I told you he *touched* me?"

"No."

"Stabbed my dog?"

"No."

"Stole my baby?"

"Nope," he points to the hallway behind me. "And there's the door? I suggest that the next time you pick up a guitar you play the damn thing. Now get before I revoke my services."

I exploit my knowledge of daytime TV runoff jargon: "But if he's an offender I have the right to know, right? Public safety stuff."

Braggert nods. "But he's not."

"Maybe he is. Just look him up and tell me that much. That's all I want."

He considers me with a stern grimace.

"You can have whatever is left in that wallet," I say reaching into my envelope. I open my wallet to prove my honest intentions, but find only empty leather.

Braggert shrugs, caught. He turns to his computer and types a few strokes, pecking the keyboard with just two fingers. The printer behind him roars to life, hums and finally spits out a sheet of paper. He hands the paper to me. "Kevin Masons isn't even the man's name," he says. "Do whatever you want with it."

I've got photo, a real name—Bradley Swanson— an address, physical description, and a short list of offenses; petty stuff, misdemeanors. Nothing more than bootlegging liquor into dry counties on Sundays.

I quickly head out the door, guessing which direction I should go, and after what seems like miles I finally come to the pawn shop. I go around back to the abandoned van to find that the thing has been gutted. No radio. No speakers. Not even a rearview mirror. I check under the seat—filthy thieves at least left Creg's notebook.

By the time I walk to the address on Braggert's

print-out the sun has set and the streets are lit by stretched dots of streetlight light. The house sits between two lights, shaded and almost dark enough to vanish. When I ring the doorbell a soft, cautious voice from the inside asks what I want.

"I'm looking for Kevin Masons," I say. "Or Bradley."

"Nobody here by that," the voice says. "Go ahead and leave, then."

Before I'm turned around, perhaps ready to forfeit to the night, the door swings open, and a small man appears in an open house coat, exposed from the socks up save the small lump of underwear hanging tight to his thin legs. He looks like me in a way; we share the same eyes. Not color or shape, but something else. "Sorry about my sister," he says. "She's a little paranoid since dad died." He steps out to the porch and closes the door behind him. "What are you looking for?"

"Kevin Masons. Bradley Swanson. Either one."

"Found and found," he says then leans close. "What are you buying? I'm stocked."

I disregard his coy smile. "Nothing," I say. "I'm here to talk about Kevin Masons. His mother."

He pauses for a moment before inviting me in—a gesture I accept with caution—and has me wait on the couch while he steps to a back room for some pants. "That's Alex," he says. "My sister."

I wave to her then shout back to Kevin or

Bradley. "I'm Jackson."

He comes back to the front room, dressed in thin, tattered slacks and white under-shirt stained yellow at the pits. He falls to the couch next to me. "So," he says, leans back into the torn cushion. "What do you know?"

"Is it Kevin Masons?" I ask. "Or Bradley Swanson?"

"Depends who you ask, I guess."

"Officer Braggert says it's Bradley Swanson."

"How do you know Braggert?" He grins, encouraged by our sudden mutual acquaintance. Alex stares at both of us, never blinking.

"We had a run-in recently. I busted up a pawn shop. Paid him for his services, and he let me go."

"That guy's as crooked as a Catholic," he says. "He got me off, too. Small world, as they say."

He offers a drink then stands and walks to the kitchen. The floor creaks as he steps. The carpet is dirty and old, the walls filled with decorative statues and photographs. The statues, small and white. The photographs are varied and represent thirty, maybe forty years by judge of deterioration and clothing styles. Every face is a smile. "No," I say. "I just want to know how you know Kevin Masons."

He brings back two cans of beer, a brand I don't recognize, and sits this time in a chair across from me. "So you know Kevin Masons." he says.

I shake my head. "I figured you did," I say.

"Nope." He opens the beer. "I got the name from a newspaper. A few years ago."

"A newspaper?" I say.

Bradley sets his can on the coffee table between us. He tells Alex to go to her room. She leaves without argument. She is a young girl, ten, eleven maybe, brown hair, freckles, and without a single beam of sun upon her. "You're Kevin," he says. "You're Kevin fucking Masons."

I shake my head. "Only as much as you are."

"So you found the ad, too?"

I nod.

"You called?"

I nod.

He leans close over the coffee table. "But you're not the real Kevin Masons?"

I shake my head. "I thought you might be more than another fake," I say. "I figured I'd stop by on the way to her place and see how I measured up."

"Sorry," he says then returns to our shared couch. "So why'd you call her in the first place?"

"I thought she was a prostitute," I say then immediately stop to gather my thoughts. "I met this girl at a bar, she gave me her number, but I called the mother instead."

"Sexy," Bradley says.

"I couldn't tell you why I kept calling. She really seemed to need my voice, you know? She was always so excited when I talked, didn't matter what about."

"Sounds familiar," Bradley says. "She was the same way when I called."

I grab the beer, take a few sips for the thought-time, then ask, "Why'd *you* call?"

"Our mother died, Alex and mine. Some disease or something. I was pretty young and Alex was just barely two. Then our dad got killed a few years back just a couple miles from here on the way home from work. We were left with nothing. When I saw the ad I thought maybe I could fool Alex, get her really talking again, but then I fell into it. I figured Kevin Masons had his reasons for leaving. I had mine for taking in the slack. Nobody is hurt." He finishes off his beer, takes mine from my hand and starts in on it. "I used the name as an alias a few times. Once to Braggert. How's she measure up to your mother?"

"Mine left," I say. "A while back. We don't talk."

"Both of us without a mother," he says leaning back. "What are the odds?"

I'm beginning to think, *pretty good odds.*

Bradley stands and announces that he has to piss, exhales a soft *excuse me*, and grabs his dick with heft as he steps over my knees.

I am sitting in a stranger's living room, sinking into a couch that wraps around me, still tasting a beer I've never heard of—loving the taste, really—and why doesn't any of this feel weird? Why does this couch open for me? Why do all the photographs along the walls frame smiles?

The toilet flushes, and when Bradley stomps through the door he is laughing. "Wait," he says. "So you were just going to show up? You were just going to knock on her door and stand there with open arms and you never once thought she might realize you aren't her son?"

"I guess not," I say. "I thought, why not see who she really is?"

"But when she sees you she'll know you aren't Kevin. Voices can get confusing over the phone after time and distance, but she won't forget a face."

"I'll lie and say I was in an accident." I lift my stocking hat and show where I once had an ear.

Bradley's eyes widen. "She'll shit when she sees that."

"Maybe this whole trip isn't really for her, then," I say.

He rides a nod for a stretched moment before speaking. "Can I come?"

Before I answer he's already slipping on a coat.

"What about Alex?"

"She'll be fine," he says. "She's survived so far."

If I knew her for any history at all I'd say she's adapted to her life without parents. She greets every hope as ephemeral and embraces every disappointment like it's just one more piece of her life going the way it always has, always will. And the walls around her, the couch, the great volume of stale air, dominates this small child. She watches us step to the porch, watches her bother slowly close the door, and the last image I get is of her looking just as she did when I first came into her life as a stranger. We climb into Bradley's pickup truck and drive away.

NINETEEN

Flaming Hair and a Tattoo

During his legally employed days Bradley Swanson was a butcher at a local grocery store, but he couldn't handle it. It wasn't the blood or the death or even the OSHA regulations and union; he said, "It was the fuckers who came in thinking they knew the difference between tripe and cow tongue, or rump roast and brisket, who claimed they had an uncle or a grandfather who was a butcher during some war nobody remembers. People with six kids and a memory so cracked out they couldn't remember the names of all of them, and they come up and tell me that I needed to throw away a six-pound hunk of ground beef because of a few brown spots. That's the fucking color of meat," he says, laying on the horn for full seconds. I regret letting him drive this first leg.

Temper means passion for those without psychological disorders, Uncle Marve told me once. *For those* with *disorders, temper means about six months chained to a bed, sucking pills out from under your tongue.* Marve's wisdom has its way of peeking in at strange times.

So Bradley transferred to bread baking and home beer brewing, both of which he admits might have been a status downgrade, but "nobody," he says, "gets mad at a brewer." He started with beer but quickly moved to liquor. Bootlegged into dry counties then went to jail. He didn't stay long though. He pinched officer Braggert out of a technicality that states home distilling isn't a felony if made for personal use; only a misdemeanor, though Bradley brags that his operations supplied over a dozen counties. In return for his services Braggert got free booze and a place to crash whenever he needed either. "And I've got his number," Bradley says patting his wallet, "if we should need it."

Then I tell him everything about me, from the want-ad all the way to Robert the bodybuilder, and even about Creg who by this time might be sitting in a jail cell of his own, might be sitting at Luisa's. Hell, might even be happy somewhere. I pull his notebook out and toss it in Bradley's lap. "He's really the one who pushed me to go to the grandpa's will reading."

"Will reading?" Bradley says as he opens the notebook.

A detail I had forgotten. "Kevin's grandpa, he died. We have a will reading to get to in a couple days. Could've been a rich man."

"Could've been a poor man." He flips through the pages of the notebook, stopping every few to read a couple lines to himself, to look up to the road. He exhales deep after a few minutes, and hands it back to me. "Aint no way we could get anything out of that will reading without being found out."

"We could be spectators, at least," I say. "See what the real Kevin could've been."

"After we go to mom's place," he says. There's a sincere hope behind his grin.

I agree with a simple nod.

"But," he says, "If he isn't there which one of us gets to be the real Kevin?"

I shrug. "We'll worry about that later."

We are on the road for a couple hours, talking, filling each other in on these best parts of our lives—it seems unspoken for some reason that we each understand the worst parts, like we've lived kindred lives to arrive here, at this moment together—before finally we stop at a small breakfast joint just outside Clopton. I pop two Percocets. I step out, stretch. Stop. What I see in the parking lot I want to blame on a severe lack of sleep, bad pills maybe. Just not reality. Parked in front of the diner is Bodybuilder Robert's Ford Escort. I swear.

"We can't eat here," I say pulling Bradley back by the shoulder.

"Why?" he asks. "I'm hungry."

"The bodybuilder, the guy who beat the bum." I point to the small car, then survey the diner for a window, a view of Robert or his view of me. We've approached at a good spot, the side of the small brick building, and are suitably hidden unless Robert were to exit at this moment.

"Bullshit," Bradley says. "No way that 'roid freak is in there. Don't do this. I could really use some pancakes."

"I'm hungry, too," I say, "but I've seen this guy beat a man. No telling how much he liked it. I am just an escaped victim."

"What are the odds?" Bradley says, dismissing my paranoia with a confident stride into the diner. I try my hardest to trust in his confidence, to discredit the vehicle. I try to think of all the versions I've seen of this car, but any history is clouded by this current model. I could have been driving one myself, but I'm so sure this one in front of me is Bodybuilder Robert's that I say again, but this time to the empty air around me, "We can't eat here."

I sneak in, peering over the booths, examining the bodies propped upon the barstools. I see neither Bradley nor Robert, just a mix of senior citizens and grizzled men with baseball caps. Cautious, I slide up to the bar and straddle a barstool, resting my elbows on the surface. I spin a salt shaker until it spills. A waitress heeds the fall, blows the salt on my lap and shirt, and asks me what I want.

"Coffee, I think, and some pancakes."

She writes the order down, leaves me alone. Two minutes later Bradley comes out from the bathroom with sweat on his forehead. He spots me, sits down, and tells me not to go in there for a while. "I felt bad mostly for the guy next to me. That'll teach him to squat for a piss."

Bradley orders pancakes and an orange juice. He yawns and asks about the plan for the day, says, "So where is this reading exactly?" as he drums a found dirty fork against a napkin dispenser.

Still scanning the diner I tell him I don't know; that I was going to call once we hit Delaware.

"Wilmington," he says. "That's were all the credit records are kept, you know? Fuck, if someone could get rid of that fucking city Alex and I might have a fair shot at this world."

"The ''roid freak' might be into it," I say.

"We ran up nearly every credit card I could get within a month of activation. Nobody will touch me now. Can't blame them. Another problem that comes with not having family stability, I guess."

"I can't get anything either," I say, and right as I finally start to settle down out from the bathroom comes a giant calf, a giant thigh, and a thick wrist with thick fingers to match, rounding the edge of the door. Then the rest, the familiar bulk of Bodybuilder Robert, explodes through the door, nearly crushing a passing child. "Fuck. Let's move," I say, pulling Bradley from the counter. He tries to wrestle away, but I keep a strong grip.

As the bell above the door rings the waitress appears with two hot plates and Robert, I swear he does, he notices Bradley and me hurry out the door. "We'll stop somewhere else," I say as Bradley complains that my grip on his arm is drawing blood.

I wrestle the keys from him, start the truck, and we're three miles safe before I elaborate. "That was him, from the bathroom." One eye to the road, one to the rearview mirror.

"The big guy?"

I nod.

"If it makes you feel any better," Bradley says checking his own mirror, "he got a lungful of my ass in the bathroom back there."

I tell him that it does, just a little. "But not enough. I need to change something," I say. "My hair or something."

"You're paranoid," Bradley says. "He didn't see you and we got away. Slow down."

The speedometer pulls to 80, 85 ...

"Just cut my fucking hair," I yell.

Bradley takes the cue on the grounds that I pull over first. I drive a few miles down a side road until we hit an open field dusted in snow. He searches the glove box for something useful, pulling out pliers, a screwdriver, a dull butter knife—we consider it briefly— but then, stuffed way in the back he finds a cigarette lighter.

"The butter knife is looking better," I say when Bradley holds up the lighter.

"I saw this documentary once. These really fancy places in New York and Los Angeles, they burn the hair instead of cutting it. It does something with the minerals and proteins of the hair, makes it healthier, I think. Celebrities do it."

Before I can offer the obvious reasons against it Bradley is across the seat with his hands over my head and the smell of burning hair attacks strong enough to boil vomit. "Get off," I tell him but he pushes harder, says, "don't move or I'll burn your face." Robert surely wouldn't recognize me then, but the pain wouldn't be worth it.

"The fucking smell," he says wiping his nose with his shirt sleeve.

"I agree. After a few horrible minutes I push him off without much resistance. "I can't fucking breathe in here."

He tilts his head, examines his work, and says, "*I* wouldn't recognize you." He looks closer, grins. "I used to do tattoos. You need a tattoo."

"You're not giving me a tattoo," I say. "I'm fine. My hair is enough."

"No. You need a tattoo and a change of clothes."

I start the engine, rational now amid Bradley's growing frenzy. He's like a hyena, grinning so wide, and happy at the simple prospect of carving something into human skin. "I'm paranoid," I say, "but you are fucking crazy."

"I'm not crazy. You're mean."

I glance over to see him pouting, a full childish bottom lip quiver. I apologize.

"He'll never recognize you with a tattoo. You'll be somebody else entirely."

"No," I tell him, and ease the truck back onto the dirt road.

He finally gives up. Once we hit the asphalt he turns and says, "Let's at least get a little fucked up before we get back on the road."

It's been a while since I've been drunk, the day I called Kevin's mother being the latest, so the prospect intrigues me. I chew my lip for a few miles, thinking over what might not be such a bad idea, really. A day drunk sounds nice amid the anxieties of Robert, the mother, a broken arm, and all the rest so I nod, nod longer, until finally I'm sharing in Bradley's pouring excitement. I stop at the next town where we get directions to the nearest public park and grab enough beer to drown a donkey.

I'm drinking more than him. Too much more. I repeat stories of Marion and Gina, laughing through them this time as he listens with absolute dedication. "Loosen up," I think I say, and try hitting his shoulder, but miss and kiss the dirt so many times my lips swell.

I'm drinking more than him. Way too much more. I spill more stories of the parts trade, fumbling over the details like they don't matter. The stars spin fast into circles above the two of us. I eat something. Throw something up. I'm drunk and tired and drunker. I'm drinking more than him. Way too much more...

When I wake my brain follows miles behind my eyes. Then my muscles join, and finally, the throbbing in my face. My head hurts, of course, but my cheek beats heavier than any binge before. Next to me sits a broken ink pen and a needle fashioned into a dangerous looking weapon. Ink and blood stain my shirt and pant leg. My head surges.

He didn't do it. Fuck. Did he? And for confirmation I grab the rearview mirror and examine my face. Just under my right eye, big as my cheek can hold, is a jagged, poorly drawn, but still very recognizable swastika.

"Fuck, man! Now a *lot* of people will want to kill me."

I kick Bradley awake, keep kicking, through the pain in my cheek, the pain in my forehead, all the way to Bradley's pain. "Seriously, what is your problem?" He's yawning through my kicks.

"A fucking swastika." I yell.

Bradley holds his sore ribs. "But you've got your stories, right. How many other people can claim to have gassed Jews during the war?"

"I'm twenty-two years old," I yell, spitting blood.

"You can still hate them. You've organized rallies and beatings—how about that? Or maybe you have over a hundred black guys buried in your back yard. Nobody could forget you after a claim like that." He massages his leg. "Fuck man, you did some damage."

"Fix it," I say. "Change it."

"I don't know what I can do, but I'll try."

He reassembles the makeshift needle, breaks another pen for the ink, and stabs my face again, this encouraged by painful hostility. He corrects in silence until finished. "There," he says. "You haven't killed anyone and you don't hate Jews. Now what are you going to say?"

I check out the remodel. It looks like a window tilted on its point. "What the hell is this?"

"A Punnett square," Bradley says. "Now instead of gassing Jews you fucking collect biology textbooks."

When I ask, he explains that a Punnett square is a simplistic way to determine the genetic traits of offspring. Letters, representative of a specific trait for one parent, are placed on one side of the box and the letters for the other parent are placed at the top. Depending on whether the traits are recessive or dominant a couple could determine, for example, what color eyes a child might have or what color hair. A Punnett square is the beginning blueprint of a child.

"It's empty," I say. "There's no letters."

"Appropriate," he says. "No mother, no father, no referent traits."

If my parentless history wasn't obvious before, now I've got one hell of an icebreaker.

"And your bodybuilder won't recognize you now," Bradley says. "Nobody will. You don't even fucking exist."

I don't even fucking exist. Here, stretching my red skin in front of the mirror, I, for the first time I can recall look for my mother buried within my own features. My father, I've always accepted his genes by way of the work ethic we shared. Until the nail and the ear incidents we were separate bodies but with a common form. That was that. My mother, though, she's always been a peripheral being, falling outside conscious direction. Until now. Where does her face overlap mine?

TWENTY

Drawing a Father for Bradley

Every smile hurts, cracks the forming scab. Just to test the integrity of my healing skin I grin, I laugh, I make kissing faces in the rearview mirror. Bradley tells me to quit messing with it, to let it heal or "risk dying, forever to be just the dead guy with a shitty tattoo." I want to but patience has never been one of my stronger qualities. All this pain and I haven't changed. I look like Jackson Jacoby, just with face full of ink and blood, new scars in the making.

Bradley bugs me about his hunger until finally I pull into a gas station, "For nachos and a Gut Bomb," he says already salivating. I walk the short aisles, picking through single serving products like something might actually have the power to numb the pulsating in my face. Ibuprofen, aspirin, even some antiseptic wash I consider, but above all this I still have the bottle of Percocet back in the truck. I wonder about the type of people who might buy these products, the disheveled, broken bodies searching these aisles for something to keep them together until the next station, until the station following, until finally they arrive at their destination and all the weary parts and sores from the road fade in favor of the welcoming embrace of a final stop. But my Percocet stash is running low so I reconsider and accept the toll that comes with these roadway remedies. I choose Tylenol. My mother always used Tylenol. I wonder if Kevin's mother does too.

"It's on me," Bradley says and nods to the cashier to add my pills to his purchase.

As we step out the door I notice a few cans of spray paint lying loose in the back of a dirty truck. I tell Bradley to hold my pills. "I've got an idea for another buffer."

Sly, stealthy, clandestine, I step to the truck, dip my hand inside, and come back with three cans. We are on the road before Bradley even notices what I've stolen. "Why?" he asks.

"I'm building an army," I respond, grinning through the pain of my tattoo all the way to pride.

Then, for the next hour, I stop at every flat wall, visible from the road, and create the greatest armor I could possibly have. It's like recruiting a bodyguard without consent. I give credit where due: "My friend Creg gave me this idea."

On the back of a strip mall store I paint:

DEATH TO JACKSON JACOBY, SIGNED BODYBUILDER ROBERT

On a dumpster, not far from a police station I paint:

BODYBUILDER ROBERT WANTS
TO KILL JACKSON JACOBY FOR NO
REASON.

On the side of a parked van I write:

IF JACKSON JACOBY DIES, I'LL
HAPPILY TAKE THE CREDIT. MY
NAME IS ROBERT. I AM A
BODYBUILDER.

On a low highway billboard I paint a crude portrait
of Robert with the words underneath:

THIS IS ME. JACKSON JACOBY IS A
DEAD MAN. REMEMBER MY FACE
AND NAME—BODYBUILDER
ROBERT.
I DRIVE A SHITTY SPORTS CAR.
I HATE JACKSON JACOBY.
WHEN HE DIES, BLAME ME.

"If I'm dead," I say tossing an empty can to the ground, "Robert goes down with me. He'll practically take a bullet for me now."

Bradley tosses his uncapped can of paint to the ground and pulls his keys from my hand. "You're paranoid," he says, not the first time.

We take a rest where we stand, in the alley behind a small grocery store. We steal a couple milk crates and sit next to his truck, taking in the silence and the cold like they exist just for us. Then the snow starts and the pain in my cheek grows to an ache at the back on my head, then to my temples, then to the peak of my forehead. Within minutes the Punnett square is all I can think about. I want it gone. I want something to warm my face, to cover the square, but I've got nothing. I want it gone. "I want it gone," I tell him.

Bradley leans back against his truck, finishing off a cigarette I didn't see him light. The smoke from his mouth melts into the steam. "It's ink, not LSD. Calm down. That shit is permanent. As permanent as a professional job." He braves the dropping temperature, lifts his shirt above his ribs and turns to reveal a small black mess at his side. "This has been here for"— his lips move to silent numbers—"a good number of years."

I hadn't noticed it when I first saw him, half-naked at his door, but scarred into his skin is what looks like a portrait. Below, written in illegible script, is a date. "That's when my mom died," he says.

"And that's her?" I ask.

"From the only picture I found of her. Did you catch all those photos on my wall? Not a single one is of my mother. Dad always said she was more of the photographer type. She liked to organize the pictures, make them perfect, stand behind the lens just to make sure the rest of us didn't screw anything up."

Filtered by the gentle snow I lean closer and study the portrait. I'm shivering, teeth clattering, and my hands are chilled deeper by the frozen skin over Bradley's ribs, but I wouldn't pull from this moment for anything.

The portrait translates like an old cartoon, the poor characters that might have fueled the childhood of either of our parents. I'd call it homage but the lines and strokes of this mother read clearly like a genuine attempt at perfect rendition.

I nod. I ask a few questions like I'm interested in the process: "Did you trace this somehow?" "Was she really that beautiful?" "How many pens did it take?" And he answers each one with pride. The temperature continues to drop, but he bears the cold and holds his shirt high, letting me take as long as I want.

"What about your dad?" I finally ask. "Do you have one of him?"

He drops his shirt. "Not yet."

For a moment I feel like I've offended him in some way, like his father's death is a strong scab, still. I apologize. "Don't. It's not like that. I just haven't had time. With Alex and shit, I've got my time pretty much accounted for before the sun even rises."

I search for a change of subject. All I come up with is, "Can it get infected?"

Bradley glows, ignores me question. "You could do it."

I ask him what he means as I'm turning back to the truck.

"It's only fair," he says pointing to my Punnett square. "You could put my dad on my other side. I've got a picture in my wallet."

I laugh, hope he's joking, knowing he isn't, and dismiss the idea with a solid, "No."

"Come on," he says pulling out the photograph. "All you have to do is draw what you see. It's like writing but with pictures. Nothing to it."

It's not the fear of disappointing this only friend of mine that makes me cautious— judging by his current tattoo I doubt he could be disappointed with any attempt—it's instead the idea of creating something permanent. Letting something out to survive on its own in this world is a load I'm not sure I can handle. "I can't."

"It's way too cold out here. We'll go inside the truck."

"I can't be responsible for your father. A Punnett square is one thing, but a parent is something else entirely."

He completely removes his shirt. "That's not it. Having his portrait scraped into me would be like a reminder to myself that I came from somewhere. Maybe I don't like where I came from, but I still came from somewhere. I'd be okay with the picture looking like shit. In fact, I'd probably feel better about it that way."

He turns around and points. "Right here," he says. "Just let him flow over the ribs. Like waves." He laughs, his teeth chattering in the cold. He shows me how to convert the used needle and pen into a suitable gun; shows me how to break the pen so that the ink pours to a small puddle and not all over my leg.

First I scrape the skin. I drag the blackened needle along his flesh like a cat claw, going over each stroke a few times to fill the gorge with ink. He stops me after a few minutes, tells me to use poking motions. "Like a sewing machine," he says.

This new technique works surprisingly well. Drawing with dots forces an attention to detail that solid lines tend to overlook. It's the dots, the marks along the way, I guess, that matter.

I ask him to hold his father's portrait while I work. He shakes in the cold, winces with each prick causing an unsteady hold, impossible to work with. I tell him to hold still a few times, but what really does it matter? His father will be a drunken cartoon character no matter how still his son sits.

I've never created anything like a legacy. I've never added something to this world that will go on, live forever, and influence. I can feel the needle dip through layers of skin and leave behind the stain. I can smell the ink, too, sweaty and metallic. If Bradley ever has children he might lie and claim the tattoo as a prison mark. Or a drunken night with poker buddies. He could say anything he wanted to, and frankly, this scares me. "What are you going to tell Alex?" I ask. "About the tattoo?"

"I might tell her I did it. Is that cool?"

He's a good sport through most of it. Only once do I slip deep enough to fill the cracks in his dry skin with steady blood. A stack of napkins from the glove box and a few minutes are all I need to press on. When I finish I pull back and wipe excess ink from his side with a red napkin. "I think he would be proud," I say.

Bradley angles the reflective side of a CD to his new wound. He can't possibly see much of anything, but he looks for full minutes anyway and says, "You could do that shit for a living, man. I'm serious."

"It's a far move from filling vending machines."

"And a hell of a lot more permanent. This isn't just a snack."

"Thanks," I say and think again of infection. I search the glove box, under the seats, and behind them until I find a first-aid kit. I open two packets containing gauze—smells like bleach—and hand one to Bradley.

Then a man in bloody white coat steps through the grocery store doors, lights a cigarette, and as he shakes out his flame he notices a shirtless Bradley and me. The man yells, so furiously his words fall out in incoherent blocks. He hurls an empty milk crate at us, cursing as the crate thuds against the passenger door panel.

"Go-Go-Go!" Bradley yells.

I turn the keys in the ignition and stomp down on the gas. We fishtail out of the alley and are back on the open road in seconds. Back to Delaware. Back to Kevin's mother.

TWENTY-ONE

An Address

The sun doesn't look so strong hiding behind the horizon, below my eyes, below the windshield, the headlights. It grows, though, slowly. And when I hit the shoulder of the Interstate at sixty miles per hour, the tires' vibration shocks Bradley from his nap, connecting his forehead to the windshield.

"Son of a bitch," he yells. "You trying to kill us?"

"I'm pulling over," I say. "I'm tired."

Luckily I find a rest stop a few mile markers down. I see a small picnic table and vending machines but no payphones. Bradley tells me he's always thought of a payphone as "like having a family without all the burden."

He steps out of the truck, holds a fresh iodine wipe to his side. "'Cause you can call when it's convenient, and if you never want to talk to someone again you simply don't stop the truck. You just keep driving."

"We had to pull over to switch seats anyway," I say stepping around the front of the truck, eyes peeled. "I'm falling asleep."

"Why not send a letter or type an e-mail?" he continues. He finds a can of paint in the back and colors a small patch of snow. A warped cloud of fumes, colored orange by the breaking sun, rises from the nozzle.

"Sincerity and sarcasm don't translate well on the page."

"Why not Morse code?" he asks.

"You're asking a lot of the receiver."

"Send a singing telegram."

"You can't hire a guy in a cow suit to sing our kind of news."

"But the receiver is going to answer the door no matter what. Nobody will see a cow standing on the porch and not open a door. A person can pick up a phone or let it ring. A phone is all about the dialer. The receiver means nothing."

I pull back my own iodine pad, letting some fresh air on my face. "How about smoke signals?" I spot a phone just beyond the bathrooms.

"Fucking brilliant." And as Bradley disappears into the stalls, I pick up the phone, dial Kevin's mother.

She answers casual, calm. "Hello? This is Mary."

Mary. Mother has a name. I can't speak for full seconds.

"Hello," she repeats. "You've reached the Masons, this is Mary speaking."

Bradley steps from the restroom drying his hands with his own shirt. I can hear the faucet left running, whining behind him. He presses his cold face against mine, trying to absorb what snippets of the conversation he can. He motions to keep quiet, but the shivering alone is enough to distract me from this careful exchange.

"Who is this?" She asks.

"It's Kevin, mom," I say shoving Bradley away. He wrestles with his shirt, awkwardly examines his father's portrait tattoo, spinning like a dog chasing its tail. "Just wanted to check in with you."

"Kevin. I was starting to think it was one of those…"

Bradley stands back and begins to flex. He kisses his shallow muscles, smiles for invisible cameras. "Tell mom I say 'hi'," he says.

"Who was that?" she asks.

"A friend," I say. "I've brought a friend along. I hope that's okay."

She waits a few breaths. "To be honest, I was hoping we could enjoy the reunion and endure the will reading, just the family, but if he's already this far across the country I couldn't turn him down now, could I?"

"You could," I say and turn back to ensure Bradley's preoccupation. "It could be just the family if you want." I watch Bradley kneel into giant lunges, open his mouth to catch some snow, and pee on a bush, all in one seamless motion. He has years ahead of me being Kevin Masons, but even with my comparably short charade I know that the real Kevin Masons would never pee on a tire.

"Are you almost here?"

"We're almost into Delaware. But we might be cutting it close getting in. What time is the reading? And where did you say it was?"

"Of course," she says. "Let me find it."

As she shuffles papers in the background I pull out a chewed ballpoint and Creg's notebook. I flip to a random page, shuffling through Creg's search. She gives the address, some town I don't remember seeing on the map—too small a town to mean anything to cartographers, I guess—and a time to be there tomorrow, one o'clock. "I'll be there," I say and smack a kiss through the receiver.

"You don't have to leave," she says. "I'd love to chat for a while."

"Okay." A few seconds pass in silence. "So, how was your day?"

"Good," she says. "It's been crazy getting this reading organized. You'd think all it would take is a few letters and a rented room with a VCR, but it's so much more than that."

"Like what?" I ask.

I watch Bradley do jumping jacks, his dick exposed and flopping with each bounce. "Come on," he says, unable to contain a laugh.

"The lawyers for one thing. They jump on any kind of property exchange. Grandpa should've had this taken care of a long time ago."

"I've heard about laywers—"

"Let's go," Bradley yells, sticking his head inside the door. "I'm freezing my dick off out here."

I cover the mouthpiece. "Then go in the truck." He instead approaches me, stands right behind me.

"And the moving trucks," she says. "We have no idea how many to rent for all of it."

"That's a lot of stress. Now don't wear yourself out, okay?"

"Seriously, I can't bend my fingers," Bradley yells.

I turn away again. "Shut the fuck up," I tell him. "I'm talking."

He pouts behind me, whispers "She's not your *real* mom," and for some reason that infuriates me. I tell Kevin's mother I have to go, that a small child is choking, over-enunciating at "small child," and slam the phone down. My anger at Bradley transferring through the phone and who knows what Kevin's mother thinks now? If I had any more change I'd call back immediately and apologize. I stomp off toward the truck. He follows silently like a scolded child.

I turn around. "What the hell was that?" I yell. "Get in the fucking truck if you're so cold. Where would we be if we weren't going to this fucking reading? Who would we be? We would be two strange fuckers without families." Slow steam escapes from my mouth.

Under his breath, so quiet I sense his remorse even before the thought fully forms: "I have Alex," he says.

I swing, connect, crack the tattoo on his sore ribs, perhaps finally snapping one. He drops to the ground, but stays only long enough to prep a fist for my own ribs. I'm down. I'm beaten. I weep like a fucking child. The tears freeze before offered the chance to drip from my face. "Get in the fucking truck." I then flex my cheeks so hard the scab from the empty Punnett square breaks. The blood burns slow in this cold winter, thaws the tears to decorate the snow in transparent crimson.

Bradley allows me a few moments before apologizing and offering to help me up. "Are you crying blood?" he asks, kneeling now to my level.

"Crying for blood, I think."

TWENTY-TWO

The Motherless

For the first few miles of the final leg into Delaware we are silent, so silent we can hear the snowflakes die against the windshield. We can hear the slush rip from the road under the truck tires. We each hear the hectic unease of mutually confused breath. Breaking the silence Bradley finally says, "If he's got a jet ski I get it." He rubs his sore hand.

"That's not how it works," I say, my ribs now aching. "The grandpa has already divvied his stuff. The reading is just where we find out who gets what."

"I know," he says. "I mean, if Kevin Masons gets a jet ski I call it."

"We're spectators," I remind him. "They'll know we aren't Kevin Masons."

Bradley pulls down the visor mirror, checks his newest tattoo. He takes a napkin from the glove box, spits in it, and wipes the tattoo clean; he scrubs for straight minutes, winces at the pressure. This truck is thick with our stale breath, the two of us have been breathing in each other's air long enough to surface miles of tense hostility, but I can accept this. What I fear is that his cleaning has devolved into attempted removal. We're like brothers, in an odd sort of way, and the tattoos, they mean something.

"It's clean," I tell him, peeking at his struggle. He says nothing.

What brings us back to brothers is entering Delaware. We share a hushed smile and both of us are scanning the road for signs. We are headed to Pliskow, a small town outside Newark. "Small town." Those are Kevin's mother's words. And she wasn't exaggerating. I know small towns—I've lived in them since birth—but this place is three-houses-and-a-post-office small. Tucked back behind a tiny bend of trees sits a church, the address for the reading. In the dark the building blends into the surrounding foliage.

"We'll find a motel," I say, "then come back tomorrow as sad as we can try to be."

As I pull away from the church Bradley leans to me and says, "I don't have anything black to wear."

"We'll shop around," I say. "We'll find something great."

After an hour of wandering roads we happen upon a small motel. When we ask, the lady at the counter tells us we are eight miles north of Pliskow. I ask for return directions before braving the cold night once more, before falling into the warmth of a real bed. A real pillow. Real blankets. She says, "It's easy," and draws for me a crude map on the back of a pamphlet. "Must be something big going on that way. We've had a few check in, heading that way tomorrow."

I just nod, thank the woman, and retreat into the cold.

The room reminds me of the room I had as a child, drab walls and heavy, dirty curtains. Or maybe it's just the occasion tricking me.

We spend that night, until sleep, meshing game plans, going over the rules of a will reading. We improvise most of the formalities, laughing through yawns at the ridiculous rituals we conjure. Bradley tells me that kissing the widow on the neck is an expected way to offer condolences. I tell him that if anyone is wearing red the mourners are allowed to set fire to his hat. He says he knew that and adds that in New Guinea all property is burned in sacrifice to the estate gods. We both laugh, fall asleep fast, like camping in a front yard.

We wake up late. The sun draws to its peak and the woman from the counter is banging on our door, yelling that checkout was at noon. Bradley and I look to each other, simultaneously mouth, "Noon," knowing the hurry we've got to be in to get to Pliskow by one o'clock. Grabbing what little belongings we have I check the clock on the nightstand: twelve-forty. We rush out the front door, destroying the morning snow with our bare feet.

I'm wearing a T-shirt I picked up from one of the diners somewhere back west, with the GreenAmerica uniform pants, filthy and worn thin by these days of sweat. Bradley says the pants smell like Keith Richards looks. Bradley has on a pair of dirt-spotted jeans, a little league baseball shirt he said used to belong to his nephew, and no socks or shoes. He's the first to say it, but we both think it: "We aren't wearing black."

"No time," I say. "A funeral, though—I think a funeral is where you have to wear black. You can wear anything to a will reading."

"Sure?"

I'm not sure, but I say I am.

The church looks the same during the day—a bit of light added, sure—but my unease is so strong it clouds my eyes. I pretend as hard as I can that something good can come of this.

I squeeze the truck between two compact-cars. The lot bursts with vehicles of all kinds, classes of all types. We follow a few feet behind a short man, twenty-eight maybe, though his head holds little hair. He's dressed in slacks and a clean white T-shirt.

We walk to the back of what feels like a congregation of all boys. Boys, my age and some younger, some older, and all with homely attempts at presentation. Most wear dirty clothes. Some have pressed pants and collared shirts. One man wears an old suit, much too small for his large frame. At the front of the room sits a TV on a particle-board stand with an abused late-80's VCR underneath. Bradley and I find a seat at the back of the crowd.

"There's no girls," Bradley whispers to me. "And I

don't see any property up there. Shouldn't they have the stuff up there to hand out?"

I shrug. "That's okay, you aren't wearing any shoes."

"Fuck. I'm hittin' the Lost and Found," Bradley says. "Hold my seat."

He steps up, pardons his way through three silent sets of legs, and disappears, his bare feet padding through a hallway behind me. The room warms, so many bodies just perhaps as anxious as me. I scan the area for a thermostat, seeing only a field of nervously bowed heads—prayers maybe, but nerves definitely. I'd speak, but I'm afraid my voice couldn't ring loud enough for this deaf crowd, all of them uninterested in me, Bradley, nothing but that VCR.

Full feet of air separates every person in this room. The distance doesn't feel accidental. Every person seems to understand the lifelong understanding of being alone.

I can hear a toilet flush and moments later Bradley strides in wiping his hands on his pants. He sits down, leans close. "You'll never fucking believe this," he says.

I look down at his feet and spot a pair of white loafers. "Nice shoes."

"Robert. He was in the bathroom."

I sweat.

"What the fuck, right?" Bradley flashes a smiles.

The Punnett square itches as I get hot. My singed hair begins to stink. "Did he recognize you?" I ask.

"He was just washing his hands, thinking hard about something it looked like. He's got this vein…"

"What the fuck is he doing here?" I barely contain my panic.

Bradley tells me to shut up. He says to get over myself, says again "You're paranoid," and reminds me that Robert did mention a recent death in his family out east. "You said that, right?"

"What are the odds?" I say. *Pretty good odds*, I think.

Robert thunders from the hallway behind us. Without tensing my neck I strain my eyes to catch as much of him as I can. He walks behind us, clicks down the center nave, heel, toe, heel, toe. Everyone here sweats to his step. When he lands at the first pew he pardons his way past a few dwarfed boys and sits quietly. It's Moses and the Red Sea.

He sits a room away from me yet he's not once been further than a thought since our episode back in Ohio. What is he really doing here? What really are all these boys doing here? Each hoards his personal space like the fight for it has been ongoing since birth. They take comfort in distance, a feeling I understand well. Eventually, after so many minutes of stoic silence, a single boy gathers strength, quickly scans the room, then retreats back to his nervous bow. Then another. More heads pop and turn, retreat. A field of twinkling stars they are, exploring their limits, searching for what makes them happen. Who gives them life, reason to be here?

More heads move, build to waves, until one body stands, walks to the back of the church, and exits without ceremony; just muffled steps against the worn carpet. More boys follow. The survivors endure a silence for a while before two more boys leave. This clunky emptying of the church has each face looking progressively more distraught. A few carry tears and few hits walls. How far did they come? What distance justifies their desertion?

This entire time Bradley remains silent. I too, don't speak a word, because no word could mean more than all these boys giving up.

The sun is just starting to melt behind the horizon. Stained glass windows turn from rose to crimson. Four of us left, then a boy with a baby face and a coat three sizes too big stands and shuffles his way out into the snow.

"What now," Bradley whispers. "If we leave now we might get out without Robert noticing."

I say nothing. I just watch the large man up front sitting so still he could be asleep. Bradley coughs loud, forced. Robert jumps at the sound. He yawns, stretches, then takes two quick glances down either side of his empty pew. Stained glass crimson bleeds to velvet by the still-dying sun.

"Let's go," I say, begin to stand. My knees and ribs ache at the stress.

Robert suddenly leaps to his feet. His stand freezes

me. He slowly walks to the TV, stops. He bends down, checks the VCR. "Fuck, you," he yells and in one swift move lifts the entire set and slams it against the floor. It doesn't smash the way I thought it might. It bounces, cracks a bit, but endures the rage. Its defiance seems to anger him even more. He kicks it, like me might a bum in barn.

Robert spins hard to leave but stops when he sees us huddled in the back row, as shocked as he. He stares for a moment, then smiles and runs to me with his arms open.

Bradley and I both scream.

"Jackson," he yells. "Jackson Jacoby." I accept his grand hug and grin as he gives my new look a once over. I would run but where would I go?

"Robert," I say. "I can't believe this."

He runs his hand through my hair, traces my Punnett square with his enormous finger. "What the hell is all this? You queer now?"

I give Bradley a quick pursed grin, then turn back to Robert and laugh the comment away. I introduce the two men. They shake hands and together we sit.

The world doesn't make sense yet, but I jump to fill what gaps I can. "You know Kevin Masons?" I ask. His expression goes blank. I turn to Bradley and he's got the same look. "I'm beginning to wonder if the boy even exists."

Bradley looks out over the empty church, the nave once full of believers, now emptied of all but the desperate. "This can't be a joke," he says. "This can't be a fucking joke."

Robert looks ready to faint. He relaxes into the pew and reaches into his suit's inner pocket, pulling out a thin piece of grey paper. "I guess you guys have seen one of these."

It's the want-ad, the plea for Kevin Masons to return home. The cry of a desperate mother hoping for a desperate son. But not from *The Veranda View*, from some paper called *The Herman Essex Area Dispatch*.

Robert takes the want-ad, folds it delicately and slips it back into his pocket.

Bradley climbs upon the pew, sits on the backrest. "So all of this was a witch hunt? Just to see who would lie about being Kevin Masons?"

Robert shrugs. "Or maybe to see who would really want to be Kevin Masons."

All of us shiver. The air outside bleeds in from separated joints and gapped doorframes. The windows dull to black. "We need to find the mother," I say. Without a word more the three of us stand and exit the cold church.

"There was no tape in the VCR," Robert says as our feet fall into the snow tracks of so many quitters before us. "I have rage issues because of the steroids, but honestly, I would have busted the thing even without all the extra testosterone."

"You did the right thing," I say and the three of us squeeze into Bradley's beaten truck.

TWENTY-THREE

Road Weary as We

I am allowed, though rarely, to experience hope. I am able to ride the ebb and flow of promise and disenfranchisement. I've handled it well over the past days though the time comes when buoyancy by the uncontrollable natural laws no longer satisfies. The truck still stinks of spent hair. Past the gauze, past my shirt, to the grey upholstered seats my blood stains brown. We're driving toward Kevin's mother, though, and that's all that matters.

We all think it but none of us voice the doubt: if Kevin Masons isn't real then the mother might not be real either. The mother might just be another hope we must accept as destroyed. Afterwards we might have to spread our way, the three of us pseudo-brothers, out across the country where we belong. We'll promise to keep in touch, but with the way our voices might sound through a phone, shredded by the static of a bad connection, none of us will intend to keep that promise. Hearing our voices will only bring back the sound of rubber to road, of wind whistling though a cracked windshield, of hollow knocks on unanswered doors.

But the first payphone, the first phone book, and there she is: Masons, Hue and Mary, hidden within so many hundreds of other families.

"We'll just show up," Bradley says. "We'll knock on the door and if she doesn't open we'll bash through it. We deserve that much. We traveled all this way."

"We're the liars," I remind him. He quiets, leans against a wall, licks his lips. "But your way's about all I can think of," I add.

The house is smaller than I had expected. The others agree. "I pictured a mansion," Bradley says. "Or at least three stories," Robert says, "with some fancy Spanish shingles or something."

In this dark it's hard to tell much about the house other than its size. The color might be white, it might be some shade of blue, or it might be red. Nothing is permanent right now. The driveway sits empty and upon realizing this Bradley says to us, "looks like nobody's home. Maybe she travels a lot, for business or something."

"Not with this house," Robert says. "She works the graveyard shift with a house like this."

Then I say, "Maybe she doesn't need a big house. Maybe she's alone in there and all she needs is a place for her and her husband and a room to watch TV."

Robert tells Bradley to park the truck along the curb just outside the house. Bradley obeys without question. The truck rocks hard into park, and the three of us pile out onto the street. "Okay," Robert says. "I can get in just fine, but I'll need the two of you to keep watch."

We nod together as Robert slips somewhere behind the house, made easier by the absence of streetlights. We've got a bit of light from a little grocery store on the corner, the sign out front advertises to this entire block, but other than this small trickle we are left in the dark. Bradley smiles. I can't help but envy whatever light he's got inside him. "I'll bet she is beautiful," he says.

"Of course," I say. "Like an angel."

"I bet she will make us dinner. Or cookies, or something. She'll hear how far we traveled, and we *were* the ones who stayed the longest. She probably makes a great casserole."

His eyes are glazed by the grocery store light. They have a sheen to them, a film I'll call tears. How long as he wanted this mother? Has it been longer than me?

I open my mouth to agree, but from the front door bursts Robert, grinning, shushing us with his thick finger. The two of us slide up to the door, try peeking around Robert's girth. "Wait," he says. "It's dark and I don't know if anybody is home. Just be careful."

We nod, cut around him, and Bradley has the living room light flicked on before Robert can stop him. We see the world around us as ours.

I won't say that I am disappointed by what I've been given. The walls are sturdy and the refrigerator is full, I'm sure, but the paint falls from those walls in large chips and the food smells rotten even from the

227

living room. It's a house. But I wanted a home.

"Look here," Bradley whispers. He points to a shelf full of portraits and framed photos. The wall next to it, too, is covered with people. I pull one from the shelf, a larger photograph, packed with people standing shoulder over shoulder. It might be a family reunion. It might be a ribbon cutting ceremony for the opening of a family business. It might even be a funeral wake. The faces and the clothes reveal a diverse emotional pool. But one thing is similar. They all have the same eyes.

Robert grabs the photo from me, slicing my thumb on the cracked edge of the glass—but I keep quiet—and says, "that one's got to be her." He points to a petite woman standing near the center of the crowd.

Bradley rushes over. "How can you tell?"

"Look at her," Robert whispers. "She's beautiful. She's got a great body. And you can see how much she strains to smile. Any mother with a runaway would find it hard to smile." He pulls the photo closer to his face. "See, right there she's thinking, *What did I do wrong? What caused my own blood to desert me like he did?*"

I take the photo back. "You don't know that. Maybe she was a fine parent but Kevin was a screw-up. Maybe his leaving was a great thing for both of them."

"Then what the hell are we doing here?" Robert says turning back to the photographs.

Bradley pops out from a room in the hallway, mists the air with a spitty bird call. When Robert turns to leave I slide the photo free from the glass and stuff it into my back pocket. I steal another look to the wall of photographs. Having seen this petite mother of mine I can't help now but pick out her image in all the other pictures. They jump to me; in one at a birthday party, in another with her hand to the camera, shy, in another kissing who might be Kevin's father. In another she holds what might be an infant Kevin. I step up to this picture, pull it from the wall, and it too goes into my pocket.

The hallway smells of mold. I run my finger along the wall, pulling away a thick coat of dust and dirt. I fight hard to swallow back a cough. "What's in here?" I ask.

"Look around, stupid," Robert says. He apologizes for the name-calling, citing the steroids once again for the outburst. "It's Kevin's room."

It is. Here is where he slept. Here is where he dreamed. Here is where he made plans to run away, to flee this very room. Posters decorate the walls like any other son's walls. Clothes and junk claim the floor. Drab, green walls and heavy curtains. "Like my room," I say. "At home my walls were green."

"This *exact* green," Bradley says. "Or just a similar green. Because my room is pretty close to this color. Maybe even exactly this color."

I back down. "Maybe not this exact shade, but I'd say it is pretty close."

Then Robert steps between us with a stuffed dog. "I had one of these. Mine was a Doberman, but I think it was the same brand."

Bradley holds up a handheld video game system he claims he had when he was seven.

Robert comes to the center of the room with a book he claims his father read to him when his was sick with chickenpox.

I find a pair of boots I think I remember my mother buying for me one winter.

"I had sheets like these," Bradley says.

"I had this shirt," Robert says.

And just to top them both I hold up a baseball trophy and say, "I won one of these when I was sixteen," though I never played baseball.

The tension between us, this useless hostility, fills Kevin Masons's dusty room tight enough to suffocate. We are breathing this lie, drowning in this pointless destination and all of us—we all break under the weight of understanding. Like an open window the room cools.

Then from further back in the house an alarm clock sounds. The three of us panic, trample the shattered mess we've made of Kevin Masons's room, but instead of running to the front door, Robert turns toward the alarm. Bradley follows. And I am right behind both of them.

She is pressed against the furthest wall, crying, destroying every item on a dresser in search of a weapon, or a phone, or even a window latch. This first live, flesh and blood, image of Kevin's mother is of a woman terrified. "Get out," she yells. "Get out of my house. My husband is on his way home."

None of us speak. She *is* the woman from the photos—Robert, I know is quietly wallowing in that small victory—but she is so much older. The stress of a lost child has eroded cracks into this stone woman. The alarm still screams.

Finally, I speak as best I can. "Mary?" I say. "Mary Masons?"

She tightens. She stays facing us, but the hunt for something blunt continues unhindered behind her. Before speaking she pulls a large candle from behind her back and raises it for attack. "What do you want?" she asks. She sounds willing to offer anything.

I step a bit forward. "We're your son," I say.

She relaxes slightly, still holding the candle white-knuckle tight. "Kevin?" She looks to none of us specifically. We all three nod.

I notice then that all three of us have our hands held high to show our passive nature, though *I* wouldn't believe us. I can't blame Mary for staying on the defensive.

"You went to the will reading? All three of you?"

"There were more," Robert says. "The church was filled."

She lowers the candle to her chest. "I went there. There was nobody."

We all three nod. "We were the last ones," I say.

I should be angry. I should demand an explanation—why were we conned into driving across the country? Why was there no death? Why was there an entire church full of Kevin Masonses? But watching her quiver with an impending explanation, watching her adjust her gasps to shallower breaths as the three of us become a landmark in this shared moment of our soldered lives is more than enough to waive any reason. We have arrived. "We hoped we would see you."

She returns the candle to the dresser, walks slowly to the wall. She flicks a light, the three of us shield our strained pupils, and by the time we refocus Mary is in our faces. I straighten my back, flex my cheeks, and check my teeth for crumbs with my tongue.

"But none of you are Kevin," she says. "Kevin is fatter." She comes back to me and strokes my face, catches a tattoo scab with her fingernail. Her hand still gleams with cold sweat.

Her touch isn't like I'd thought it might be; I shouldn't ruin this moment with comparison.

"And you are missing an ear. Kevin has both his ears."

Robert and Bradley stifle laughter.

"So you are the only three who stayed?" she asks, slight desperation.

We nod, look to each other, unsure of what comes next. "Torch accident," I say. "From when I was younger." I can still feel the dew from her fingers.

"Did you see a boy …" she says, stops and turns to dresser drawers still open from the weapon search. Pulling out a stack of photos bound with a rubber band she finishes "… who looks like this. He's older now, but he probably still looks pretty much the same. His father and I are pretty worried."

I take the photos, look at them one by one, without learning a single face. Through the entire stack I'm thinking how it might feel to light each image on fire. Or if I would even feel at all. I'd be destroying and that's all I really want right now.

For years after my head injury I felt that missing ear throb. When I became embarrassed I could feel the blood pool. When punched during the heart of winter it stung. The ear was still a part of me. Even after I accepted that it was gone I could still feel wax build up inside. Now though, all these years later, I realize a new ear wouldn't be an ear at all.

I give the photos to Robert, maybe to Bradley, and Kevin's mother steps close, like she needs to search every twitch of my body for a clue to the only thing that matters to her. "Yeah," I say. "From that photo of the beach. He was there."

She hugs me, grabs me by the face, kisses me. Those cold hands have their warmth.

She asks if I talked to him, if I knew where he might be now, if I got his phone number by chance, and to the other two fake Kevins behind me she searches for hope. They shrug, shake their heads, look closer at the pictures. "I saw him in the parking lot," I say, "when I went out to smoke. They didn't see him."

Robert jumps quickly on my claim. "I might've

seen him," he says. "I thought I saw that guy when I was in the bathroom. I was checking the symmetry of my pecs. I'm a bodybuilder."

The mother nods, her interest obviously superficial, but Robert glows anyway.

"I *would have* seen him," Bradley contributes. "But I was on the phone most of the time. I take care of my younger sister all by myself. I had to make sure she was doing fine without me."

She offers the same feigned interest.

Robert comes back: "I had to care for my brother for a while. He joined the Air Force, though, and now he fights. God bless him, I say."

"My sister wants to join the military," Bradley says, "but I want her to do something more important. I think she should be a mother. What's more important than that?"

Through all of this Kevin's mother offers the most convincing fake sincerity I have ever seen. I'd thank her for this audience, for this moment to let them tell the stories of their lives to the only ear they've ever wanted, but I can't. Like I could genuinely lose something to this family if I remained silent I cut through the noise with my own reason for love: "I stole a guy's ear."

All the noise stops for a moment, just a moment, before the gap fills with the flood of greater conquests. Robert says he collects tongues. Bradley says he once bit off a dog's tail to save a sea otter. Robert says how much sea otters contribute to the water pollution and quotes some figure from some made-up scientist. Bradley claims he knew about the sea otter theory and adds that the study was later rejected by a panel of marine biologists who blah, blah, blah.

They top one another for full minutes, and Kevin's mother, me, we are silent. We touch glances once or twice, pulling away quickly because of how strange this situation is to both of us. I don't know if there is much to win here, but I know that I am losing. I think of something great, a story worthy to the title *son*, but as I open to let it out she raises her voice above all others. "I'll call the police," she says. Her words might echo if her home weren't so soft.

To this one person whose respect would make all the stories of conquest and control worth every breath, worth every word they steal from honest existence, I am nothing. Will she tell of me to a neighbor with a new car, to a sister with a new baby? Probably not. I am not even a story she could tell to some distant grandchild. I am an intruder one phone call from a jail cell. I might, at best, be a story of near-murder to her. She might be the same to me.

Robert calls her bluff, states that this room doesn't even have a phone. "And the only exit is behind us," he says.

I tell him to stop. I tell them both that we should just go. "We aren't wanted."

The mother is sliding away. She has the candle poised again as a weapon and moves so slowly only I notice the shift. Robert and Bradley argue amongst themselves about coming all this way. "You are such a liar" they each say, three times, maybe four though no accusation overpowers another.

"And my husband will be home soon," Kevin's mother repeats. "He doesn't like strangers and he, even more than me, wants Kevin home. If he sees you here, he might just do something bad to you."

"Like what?" Bradley says, dismissing the threat.

"He's real big," she says. "He keeps a gun in his car, too. He's trained with it."

Robert steps close to her, backs her into a corner. "All a gun can do is kill us."

"Let's go," I say again. I swear I hear an engine throttle outside.

"Aren't you even a little upset?" Robert yells. "We came all the way across the country on a fucking witch hunt. She knew Kevin wouldn't see one of those ads. She needed us just as much as we needed her. She's crazy."

Bradley leans against Robert. "She's a fucking liar," he says. "A fucking liar."

"Let's go," I say, though I nearly whisper it.

"No. We deserve answers. What really happened to your son?" Robert asks. "Did you kick him out? Did you just up and fucking leave him?"

"You're a goddamn liar," Bradley repeats.

She wants to cry. I can see her face strain, can see it flex to pull tears and open wide for screams, but she can't.

"No wonder he ran away," Robert says. "I would've done the ..." but he can't say it. We all freeze. Headlights pour through the bedroom window and the heavy, rusted door of an old car slams shut just feet away. Like filthy rats we run.

We flee through the back door, disappearing behind a neighboring house and make our way to Bradley's truck as best we can in this foreign block. We're tripping over bushes, over each other. Bradley and Robert trade insults as we escape, a few punches too, assigning blame even as we all must understand that blame is futile. By the time we get to the truck, we are as fragmented as we have ever been.

We are miles out of Pliskow before anybody says anything more. It's Bradley and he's wiping spit from his lip as he says it, staring at me: "in that stack, there was no beach photo."

"I know," I say. "She needed the hope."

TWENTY-FOUR

The World Doesn't Bend to Smiles Anymore

*M*arion Garza told me that they offered him the job first, to lead the animals up the ramp into the kill shed. He did it for a while, tapping them on the haunches more than zapping them because he felt using shock to move the animals was an unfair way to motivate their last steps.*

"You don't even have to use the stick that much," Bradley says. "They aren't a very smart species."

We're stranded on a highway, any highway, already drifting our separate ways. No gas and no reason to keep this whole thing going. At each step, we're yelling louder to each other, fighting the noisy wind.

Marion knew that they weren't a very smart species. But that first step was always difficult. He'd prod and force and stab the animals in the hooves but sometimes the dying screams from inside the kill shed were enough to keep them stubborn. It was his idea to train El Niño, an idea that made him hate himself.

He told me all of this, crying, saying how much he wished his mother would have kept him in Mexico. He went back for a few years, boxed for a while in Chihuahua, but his father made him go back north. "You have nothing down here," he said. "You can't make me happy by getting killed in a boxing ring. Start a family. Send me photos." He didn't do either of these things. He's tried to start a family. He's tried to create valuable moments, but the closest he's even been is with Gina the lot lizard. He's still trying to impress his father, even though he doesn't exist anymore.

"You sure you don't need something?" Robert yells from behind me. "Maybe something to even you out. I know a man from Belgium without a nose who can hook you up with cheap Valium." His next breath sounds like a laugh, but the wind between us carries it away.

He worked hard to make himself into something. He had his ear, told stories of its history, and waited for the right person to take it all in, to validate his existence like his mother might. He would update her in his dreams: "I've met this woman with a great job," he would say. "I'm going on a date tonight with this girl who knows about cars," he would say. "This new one, tonight, she wants kids," he would say. His mother, dead long ago from mastitis, would fill his dreams: "You're no son of mine without one of your own."

But the thing about Marion is that he never really wanted kids. He would tell his mother that he did, but all he really wanted was a way to prove he existed. He would tell stories of his swollen ear, tell people of all the places he's gone, the people he's met and they would smile, wanting more, ready to spread his life to the open ears of others. Then more. Then more. He was never a boxer in Chihuahua, but the world wouldn't know that.

I glance back to Robert and Bradley. They are only dots tightroping the horizon.

He'd be a hero. He'd be greater than tangible. He'd be a name on the lips of a stranger, to the ear of his dead mother, eventually, and then she would realize he didn't need a family to prove existence. All he needed was the breath of strangers.

"I'll tell everyone about you," I think I hear someone say behind me. But in this brisk wind words swirl, form on their own. I turn back to check, to see who will remember me, just in time to see Creg's notebook flutter through the air from a still stretched arm in the distance— Robert, Bradley, I'm not sure. The notebook drops into the slushy brown snow in the road. I step back to pick it up, my head down to the street. The pages drip. The spiral binding twisted. The photograph of Creg's mother is separated from the book, lying in a puddle of darker slush. I gather up all the pages, but instead keep only the photograph. The rest I throw back east as I continue west.

TWENTY-FIVE

Vernon

Afat woman with three children offers me a handful of change. I tell her that if she doesn't leave I'll steal her ear. The children tear up, and she tells me I should be ashamed. "I am," I assure her. "Very ashamed."

A family, two parents, two children pass with stiff noses, and I yell to them that they should be ashamed. "I'm a person, too," I say but not even the children offer a second glance. They've been trained well to ignore the tired and lonely, to let those like us fade.

My entire body shakes cold by the end of this first day spent walking. Each step either echoes with the hard slap of slush or the dry crunch of iced snow. These sounds are my only passengers and if only they could offer direction. The one good thing about walking: if I'm going the wrong way I go it slow. Eventually, a trucker slows to a stop behind me. The driver stares into my lopsided face. He chews CornNuts and asks me through a barbecue scented haze, "what's your story?" His eyes open for me, compassion almost oozing into the flavored air.

"I steal shit." I let my breath out, a child with dreams of cigarette smoke and respect. "Body parts mostly."

"Looks like you've been stolen from." He points down at my face, tells me to turn so he can get a better look.

"I'm not fucking on display," I say.

"Point taken," he says. "Where you headed?"

"West."

"I can take you as far as the ocean," he says with a chuckle. "If you're looking to go further than that I don't want to know the reasons why."

Once inside his truck we fall quickly into conversation. I avoid the recently shorn topic of Kevin's mother and instead settle on alternating quick mentions of my ear and appreciation for this man's goodwill. Turns out, Vernon is a pretty nice guy. He'd have to be to pick up a stranger dressed in dirt the way I am—"I could get fired," he told me, "and if I do I'll invite you to the party as my guest of honor"—but he's kind in a way I haven't known for a few days. I can hear the rubber hum of progress below us.

"What do you do with the parts?" he asks. His engine warms us.

"Sell them."

"To butchers or dog food plants?"

"Museums."

"Like Dogs Playing Poker right up next to a testicle, or something?"

"Or something, yeah."

"I've seen plenty of crazy places during my runs. Not any of the parts traps like you've seen, but I know a couple. Along this road there's a good place, about four more hours west. This guy builds a maze out of snow every year around this time. Kids love it. Adults like it, too. You interested in seeing it?"

"I'm sort of busy," I lie, though the idea of a temporary maze is intriguing. "But maybe I can see it for a second."

Vernon smiles. "Next stop, Pen's maze."

We're somewhere in northern Ohio before either of us mentions the maze again. Vernon tries poking around for more conversation, tries a variety of topics, and I handle each attempt with a quiet non-response. Vernon takes each dismissal with a smile, says "I understand," more than he needs to and stays strong on this westbound road. But when we pass a billboard, fifty-five miles it says to Pen's Family Maze, I join the excitement and say "almost there," like it's the end to something. What was once only a casual stop along the road now promises a culminated life. "The final stretch," I say.

We pull into the empty lot just before the early winter night begins to fall. Vernon tells me that "movie people call this the magic hour. The shadows and the golden light," he says, "are just perfect to make every smooth feature look chiseled from stone."

Vernon gives his rig a few honks to bring the curator from the budding mounds of snow. The few falling flakes have grown now to a semi-solid blanket. From the parking lot I see a short, Hispanic man poke his way out of his infant snow walls. "We won't be ready for a few weeks, yet," he yells.

"We're just on our way through and aren't sure if we'll be back anytime soon," Vernon returns. "I figured seeing the beginning is better than seeing nothing."

The Hispanic man smiles and says he'll waive the charge like it's a generous offer. "Come on," he says. "I can at least tell you about it."

The man waves us over to the short walls. Posted at the entrance is a sign reading *Pen's Family Maze*, with a large-toothed Asian caricature smiling down. The entire spread fills, he says, maybe seventy-three hundred square feet, all tightly wound with narrow corridors and so many dead ends I already fear for the winter tourists.

The corners of the maze glow with short beams of direct light, hanging from tall posts causing the center to sit shrouded in lonely darkness, much like the rest of the world around us.

Vernon is stepping his way over the short walls and rubbing his hands together for warmth.

"How do you know where to put the walls?" I ask the man. "Do you have a plan?"

"It's different every year," he says. "Sometimes I get lost as I'm building it. I don't plan ahead. I just start piling the snow and build until people show up." He's leading me around the maze as we speak, going on about what people have said and the press coverage he's received and all the kids that have been lost to tears within the walls. We started in the dark, then made our way to a corner filled with light, where the man is able to see all of me for the first time. "What is wrong with your face," he says.

"Torch accident," I say and try to ask him another question about the maze.

"You burned it off?"

"Not me," I say. "Some guy my father knew. A long time ago. When I was a kid."

"Did it hurt?"

What kind of question is that, I wonder. Of course it hurt. Right? But suddenly forced into recollection I'm not sure how the injury felt. The nerves are healed now, just regular skin and cartilage, but then, how did it feel then? Nobody has ever before asked me if the accident hurt. "I don't know," I whisper.

He nods, still smiling, and says, "I know what you mean," and starts to drift at the thought. We begin walking again, as he continues talking. "You ever been in a car wreck? That injury, it doesn't look like a burn."

He's searching for sympathy, I think. Or communion. And I'm open to it, too. "Yes," I say, "when I was just learning how to drive." The story doesn't feel like a lie.

"My father was from Argentina, and blind," the Hispanic man says. "Not always blind, but he grew into it. Our family has built these snow mazes for as long as anyone can remember and for those few years before my father died—as he grew blind and I wasn't yet old enough to hold a snow shovel—these mazes were all failures. Nobody came." He pauses for a few beats. "Sorry about the car wreck question. I used to be an EMT. I've seen lots of burns."

Vernon kicks a short bump of a wall over with his heel and immediately kneels to rebuild.

"I'm just saying I understand failure," the curator says. "You've got to be greater than your handicap." Then he asks about the tattoo to which I respond with a shrug. The Punnett square doesn't seem to mean much these few days after its application. I can barely feel my blood throb anymore. "You should be in *The Weekly World News* or *The Inquirer*," he says. "One ear and a face tattoo—they could write something great about you."

"I love those rags," I admit. "The aliens, the deformed people. You remember Bat Boy?"

"Of course." He grins for a moment. "Let me show you something back at the house. I may have a postcard or two that you can take back with you." I follow him into his house, up on the hill only a few deep breaths away. We stomp the snow from our shoes at the front door. "Don't worry about waking anyone. I'm by myself these days."

I offer to wait by the door but he insists I follow him deeper into his house. "I haven't unpacked the back stock, yet," he says. "I've got them somewhere around here. Just lend me a few minutes."

I pull out a chair in his kitchen. Out the window I see Vernon finally realize his desertion and instead of searching for me he walks to the sheet of plastic and sits, waits. The curator's home is small, modest, with photographs filling shelves, filling every table, and hung from every wall. Most are landscapes, a few of people, and fewer still are of him. One appears to be the curator holding a machine gun. I stand to inspect the image up close but am distracted by the stacks of newsprint magazines he has leaning against the wall. Hundreds, maybe thousands, like extra end tables and flashy barstools they occupy precious space in such a small room. I examine closer, supermarket tabloids, every one of them, those rags filled with boisterous claims of quirky humanity. My mother—my real mother—used to subscribe to these magazines, would use old issues as diapers when she had to. "You weren't kidding when you said that you knew about Bat Boy."

The curator comes back with a torn box almost falling from his arms. I rush in to help. My damaged arm throbs.

"I'm a collector," he says after thanking me for the help. "These magazines give an audience to the strange and morbid. I'm a bit obsessed, sure."

He shows me a postcard of the maze taken from a three-quarter aerial perspective. The shadow of a helicopter can be seen stretched through the far end of the maze. Another postcard shows a laughing child exiting the maze. Or crying. The cold air blurs actions. A third image has the same Asian man from the front sign with the words *I was lost at Pen's Family Maze* written in large, dark letters.

I say I'll take all three and when I try to offer some money he just shakes his head and tells me, "without snow it was a wasted trip anyway."

"Let me tell you my story then," I say. "I'll use my tale as payment." I start, get all the way through one-foot Gina, Cauliflower-Ear Marion, and am just ready to reveal the parts trade when the curator interrupts:

"November, ninety-four," he says, grins wide, and turns to the fleet of boxes against his kitchen wall. He digs.

"What?" I ask, my heart building momentum. He tosses issues aside, some I swear I remember from my childhood. I can picture my mother's ashtray sitting atop a small stack, ash everywhere.

"I've got that issue around here somewhere. November of ninety-four, that was the cover story. You must not have been but six years old at the time, but I *do* remember that story; one of the craziest things *The Inquirer* came up with that year."

My blood boils with impending embarrassment, and even more than that, fury.

"A couple stealing body parts and setting up roadside museums with them. Real crazy stuff." He stays kneeling, his back to me, digging through boxes. "I know I have that thing around here somewhere."

He found me out; *I* found me out. A figment, I whisper, watching this old man dig though his collection. I've always known it was just a story, but I thought it was *my* story. I thought I brought something new to the world, but now I see that my validation was always just someone else's. Gina and Marion, they aren't real. And why am I furious? Why am I suddenly desperate for a truth that I've faked my entire life? Is it my recent history of desperation, traveling across the county for an ideal, or is it maybe that I'm simply fueled by the moment, by the curator's back to me, him kneeling ...

"I found it," he yells, turns, and I see only the cover image of a man with a missing ear before I grab the old man's neck and grip his ear between my thumb and index finger. He hasn't even the time to

251

say, "Let go," before I rip as hard as I can and he's fallen to his knees, already floating in a pool of red. I heard somewhere that it only takes eight pounds of pressure to rip off a human ear. I would have guessed five.

He screams for a few moments before fainting, convulsing a little, but not enough to worry. I search through his bathroom for some gauze and antibiotic cream but find only a dirty towel and hydrogen peroxide. I drop the supplies near him and return to the falling snow.

My life has become defined by these spurts of community followed by sudden escape. What does that mean?

TWENTY-SIX

The Tough World of Sales

There was a time, I truly believe, buried far back in American nostalgia where being a great salesman was a point of pride, where suits didn't always snub, and putting the right person into the right product implied, correctly, that there was a right person and a right product. Salesmen saw themselves as Band-Aids and Cloverine Salves, handy, simple-to-use, and effective remedies for household ills. The Purina checkerboard trousers hadn't yet become a punch line. Eager smiles weren't yet slick with greenback intentions and commissioned dreams. People were honest. A salesman was a stranger was a neighbor was a friend was a member of the family. I remember—this was before I could legibly write my name without help— my mother making me sign a Christmas card for the guy who sold us our refrigerator. That was the last time my mother held my hand. I was far too young to begin navigating this world alone.

Maybe universal nostalgia doesn't exist. Maybe

each of us carries our own personal version of the better times. It's at about twenty-two years that we all being to think of our childhood as the good ol' days and everything afterwards exists as a slow-motion face plant. The fall continues, through marriage, through career building, through parenthood, through old age, until we finally touch nose to ground. At twenty-two years old, I've just started, but I think I can already smell my own grave.

TWENTY-SEVEN

A Parent Figure with a Plan

I lost my newest Percocet refill somewhere miles back. My arm beats hard between slow pulse apexes, hurts, swells more. The cast fights back. "Slow breaths," the doctor back in Olden said if it's the only thing I haven't done to fight the pain. If pills don't work: slow breaths. If rest doesn't help: slow breaths. If pretending the arm isn't broken doesn't curb the pain: slow breaths. But the fog-heavy stink of BWP's burning blood doesn't sit well in my lungs and slow breaths might help the pain but short, quick breaths keep the stink out. *Welcome back to Veranda*. Between quick breaths I squeeze the maze curator's ear to help with the pain.

Uncle Marve told me that the greatest device the human brain ever created was the god. "It instilled the human being with a sense of purpose," he said, "to have a great parent figure with a plan." The second greatest device: the camera. The only real difference being, he said, "that a camera can't lie no matter how repulsive the subject." So it's no concern

255

then to see a small army of vans and cameras filling the park, suffocating Uncle Marve's bench. *He's preaching.*

He'd done a lot of interviews for film students needing to piece together a quick first-person history of the war. *The War.* He'd say it like it's sheer mention meant the destruction of something special. For the cameras he would tell fake stories, whine about a lost friend he never had, a bomb he "almost couldn't dismantle," or a family he sprouted overseas in some undeveloped country because, he'd say, "I was bored and we need more good workers anyway to make our shoes."

"I lied," he's told me. "But that camera never could." Somewhere out there are videos spreading the gospel according to Marve.

The vans and the cameras at his bench in the park today—no telling what they're being fed. I've never known him to capture actual television networks with his stories, but a person is bound to bloom someday, I suppose.

I pass the park, leave Marve to his congregation, and instead head to Luisa's Laundry. Despite the encouraging, gloomy weather clouds keep distant from the building, a halo they make for miles around. And in that open hole they leave, not even the sun dares pour. If only Creg would take a break. If only he would step out front, smoke, give himself a few minutes alone, I could intercept, circumnavigate the wrath of Luisa and maybe apologize for losing his notebook. But I know better. He waits inside, a fresh notebook, a copied photograph of his mother, and fingers grey with granite. I pat my back pocket, touch the original photo of his mother, and imagine how happy I will make him.

From outside, looking in through the front glass window, I can see the TV filled with English speaking news anchors. Creg never watched the news, said the faces are always the same. And he definitely wouldn't have watched English news.

Like it's another weekday with an empty vending machine to be filled I walk through the front doorway, and I step slowly to the machine. I bite my lip and wait until Luisa rounds the corner from her room in the back. "I came for Creg," I say holding my empty hands high in the air. "Not you." I'm rolling my neck in search for my friend. This place feels like a prison laundry room without him.

She flips a creased sleeve of a red shirt straight and uses her chin to fold the garment into a small packet. She adds the shirt to a large stack at her side. "You leave him behind or something?"

"Just tell me where Creg is. I'll have to leave to find him," I say to entice her.

She folds a pair of child's pants, stained at the knees.

"Did he find cable somewhere else?" I smile.

Luisa snaps the creases from a denim jacket, so

hard her forehead veins bulge. "Are you leaving?" she says.

"Maybe he's on one of your little errands. You know he got busted down at O'Malley's the last time you sent him out?"

"He told me." She pulls the shredded leftovers of a dollar bill from the pocket of some black wind pants.

"So you do know where he is?"

The news anchors on TV share a laugh, joke about something cute, a dog show or a bake sale, maybe. Must be late in the news hour.

"BWP. Did Creg get a job at BWP? I told him that place is like pheromones to Mexicans."

"He was born in the U.S," she says.

"It's a genetic thing," I say.

The news cuts to commercial, dangling the cliffhanger of a suicide story to keep the viewer conscious through the break. *Up next*, they say. *A local man found dead...*

"Just tell me where Creg is," I say. "I'll give the notebook back if that's what you want."

She steams the wrinkles from a bright orange blouse. "He went south," she says. "He thought you did too."

"Why would he have thought I went south?"

"Maybe someone told him you went that way." She smiles.

South. Into Mexico, south? "Why?" I ask. "You

didn't want him to go either. You know he won't find anything."

"And that's what he needs," Luisa says, this fake god, this guidepost behind the counter. "To know that nothing is out there. Then he can move on, start a life without his mother. Finish this life bound by her."

"You've fucked with him too much this time. You're leading him nowhere and you know it."

"What about you?" she says, sliding a plastic garment bag over a pair of black slacks. "He told me you were going to meet that lady, the mother. Why should you get the chance to see that nothing is out there, and not him?"

"It's not fair to crush his hopes like that." I sit where Creg once sat, in front of the television set. I see his cigarette butts in the ashtray, his chewed pencils laid out beside it. From this chair I see directly in front of me one of the Missing Children posters. The faces all disguised by my own penciled mustaches and devil horns, burly eyebrows and jewelry. Unrecognizable, all of them, even to the searching eye. Above the poster, atop the vending machine, a commercial plays advertising medication.

"I don't want this anymore," I say pulling out the original, beat-up, worn photograph of Creg's mother. The signature in the corner has eroded away, the name now faint and indistinguishable from the surrounding dirt. I walk to the counter. "Give me something for it. You deserve that penance."

"I've got just the thing." She pulls, from under the counter, a photocopy of a newspaper article, something that appears years and years old. The headline reads Teen Runs Red Light, Boy Dead, Mother Injured.

...to keep that woman from having a child...

"That wasn't on purpose," I say, unprovoked.

Luisa leaves the paper, untouched on the counter. "Having your ear melted off by a welding torch is a much better story, isn't it?"

I consider pulling the maze curator's ear from my pocket, showing Luisa that I don't need a fake story anymore. But I'm pulled away by the TV.

The news comes back from commercial, flashy graphics and frightening music, lead to the dangling story of a man found dead. *The body of local man, Marve Jacoby*, the reporter says, *was found dead in his home yesterday evening.*

Luisa counts quarters, stops for a moment, returns a handful to the register.

Upon prepping the body for transportation to the county coroner's office officials discovered a note under the body. The note reads, "I buried my ring in the park." I am on location at Veranda Park where officials have not only discovered the ring, but have found thousands of metal objects, ranging from coins to military shrapnel.

I leave Luisa at the counter, walk to the TV, and

turn up the volume.

Excavation crews are busy scanning the area for more metal.

Behind the anchor, behind the yellow tape, men with shovels and metal detectors examine the ground of Veranda Park. Uncle Marve's bench sits unused in the background of every shot. I've validated this man for so long, spreading his stories like a boasting parent, a proud father, and now he's gone. And suddenly, the realization of role-reversal hits hard, and I understand the validity of a parent's memory. Though Uncle Marve might never know the degree to which he was a reference point in my life, the fact remains that his was, is. "Sometimes it's more important to know something's out there and not bother with trying to find it," Uncle Marve has been known to say. You might be disappointed once you reach it."

"Who am I without the war?" Uncle Marve told me once. "Who is your Marion Garza without BWP? Who are you without Marion Garza? An old man, a sad Mexican, a lost little boy."

I turn toward the door, stopping at the Missing Children's poster taped to the vending machine. I grab one of Creg's chewed pencils, press the eraser to the poster, and remove my history.

Luisa yells to me before I reach the door. "Go back to the vending machine job. You were good at it."

"I was pretty happy doing it, too," I smile at her. "It'll be tough explaining the disappearance of their truck, though." I walk out the front door. The bell above my head rings until the closing door traps the dying sound inside.

When she doesn't think I'm watching, or maybe she knows I am, Luisa rips the photo of Creg's mother into quarters and drops the confetti pieces into a trashcan behind her counter. I rub the ear in my pocket, already thinking of places to bury it away.

JACKSON'S NAME-DROPPING CHECKLIST

How many of these references did you spot while reading *I Didn't Mean to be Kevin?*

- ☐ The Great Gatsby – F. Scott Fitzgerald
- ☐ "The Hit-Man" – T.C. Boyle
- ☐ Fight Club – Chuck Palahniuk
- ☐ "Soundbite" – Steve Aylett
- ☐ The Contortionist's Handbook – Craig Clevenger
- ☐ "Altmann's Tongue" – Brian Evenson
- ☐ "The Blue Bouquet" – Octavio Paz
- ☐ Catch-22 – Joseph Heller
- ☐ "The Garden of Forking Paths" – Jorge Luis Borges
- ☐ House of Leaves – Mark Z. Danielewski
- ☐ Kiss Me, Judas – Will Christopher Baer
- ☐ "Good Country People" – Flannery O'Connor
- ☐ The Canterbury Tales – Geoffrey Chaucer

ACKNOWLEDGMENTS

I would like to thank everyone who provided guidance—editorial and otherwise—during the writing and production of I Didn't Mean to be Kevin. Early readers Gordon Highland, Mlaz Corbier, Jason Kane, and Jamie Kiffel deserve every beer you buy for them. Rayo Casablanca and Joey Goebel deserve a few beers as well.

And you, dear reader, you're the ultimate reason for all of this. Should we ever find ourselves sharing a bar, you've got a drink on me to look forward to.

HELP AN AUTHOR

Please, click over to Amazon.com, Goodreads, Facebook, Google+, YouTube, Twitter, and any other of your online homes and spread the word of this book and of me, the author, Caleb J. Ross. Authors have no marketing budget. Therefore, we depend on readers like you to share the enthusiasm of books in order to keep our highballs full and our pints stout.

ABOUT THE AUTHOR

Caleb J. Ross has a BA in English Literature and creative writing from Emporia State University. His fiction and nonfiction has appeared widely, both online and in print. He is the author of five books of fiction and is the creator of Burning Books, a YouTube channel featuring humorous book reviews, literary skits, writing advice, and rants.

Find Caleb online:

Homepage	Calebjross.com
YouTube	Calebjross.com/youtube
Twitter	Calebjross.com/twitter
Facebook	Calebjross.com/facebook
Google+	Calebjross.com/Google

www.ingramcontent.com/pod-product-compliance
Lightning Source LLC
Chambersburg PA
CBHW020050180626
46812CB00006B/2272